Hot Chocolate Wishes

Pier 70

Reckless
Fearless
Speechless
Harmless
Clueless

Primal Instincts

Chase (Volume 1-3)
Capture (Volume 4-6)
Claim (Volume 7-9)

Heroes & Havoc

(Sniper 1 Security, Devil's Playground, Southern Boy Mafia)
Wait for Morning
Beautifully Brutal
Without Regret
Never Say Never
Beautifully Loyal
Without Restraint
Tomorrow's Too Late

Standalone Novels

Unhinged Trilogy
A Million Tiny Pieces
Inked on Paper
Bad Reputation
Bad Business
Filthy Hot Billionaire
RULE

Naughty Holiday Editions

2015
2016
2021

Hot Chocolate Wishes

The Jamesons of Coyote Ridge, 1

NICOLE EDWARDS

NICOLE EDWARDS LIMITED
A dba of SL Independent Publishing, LLC
PO Box 1086
Pflugerville, Texas 78691

Copyright © 2023 by Nicole Edwards Limited

This is a self-published title.

HOT CHOCOLATE WISHES
The Jamesons of Coyote Ridge, 1

COVER DETAILS:

Image: © aturshina (135410922) | 123rf.com ; © photostio (97837483) | 123rf.com ; © fabrikacrimea (109132783) | 123rf.com
Design: © Nicole Edwards Limited

INTERIOR DETAILS:
Formatting: Nicole Edwards Limited

AUDIO DETAILS:
Narrators: TBD

ISBN: (ebook) 9781644180921 | (paperback) 9781644180938 | (audio) 9781644180945

BISAC: FICTION/ROMANCE/General | FICTION/LGBTQ

Dedication

To the fans of the Coyote Ridge Universe.
You humble me every time you ask for more. Thank you.

One

Thanksgiving night…

"TATE! DON'T FORGET THE ORNAMENT BOX!" REILLY Jameson yelled loud enough for Tate Riggs, her best friend/roommate, to hear from up in the loft space they used as a makeshift attic.

"Which one?" he shouted back.

"The one with the ornaments," she muttered because she had no idea.

When they'd taken down the decorations at her parents' house last year, Reilly had been too upset to pay attention to the ones her mother set aside to give them when they moved into their new place. If she had to guess, her mother hadn't paid much attention either. Their hearts had been too heavy to deal with much of anything.

But she wasn't going to think about that now. This year, the entire family vowed to keep their spirits up. Reilly knew it wouldn't be as easy as it sounded, but she would certainly try.

To prove it, she was starting by kicking off her annual tradition of decorating the tree now that they'd scarfed down turkey, dressing, and a ridiculous number of pies, signifying that Thanksgiving was officially over. She'd even bypassed a second piece of pumpkin pie to ensure she wasn't too full to move.

Of course, she'd snuck a couple of additional pieces when her mother wasn't looking and put them in Tupperware so she and Tate could have breakfast tomorrow morning.

The kettle whistled on the stove.

"I'm makin' the hot chocolate," she yelled to Tate.

"Make mine a double," he called, sounding as though he was no longer buried deep in their boxes of crap.

"A double. *Pfft*. Like I would ever be that stingy."

After pouring the hot water over the powdered chocolate in each cup, Reilly stirred and added a generous helping of Bailey's chocolate liqueur. Next came the peppermint candy canes. She stuck one in each cup, then shoved her hand into the bag of miniature marshmallows and grabbed a handful. She held her hands over the cups and let the little white puffs of sugary, airy goodness rain down onto both cups, grinning as they piled up and tumbled onto the counter.

She was drizzling chocolate syrup when Tate finally appeared, huffing and grimacing as he carried two enormous boxes and one smaller one in his arms.

"Take one," he grunted. "Please."

Reilly set down the chocolate syrup and rushed over to help her best friend.

"Tell me one of those is the right one," he said when she relieved him of the small box before grabbing one of the larger ones.

"Probably."

Tate dragged the lid off the box he had set on the coffee table and sighed. "Not this one."

Reilly leaned over to look in the box and laughed when she saw the ugly Christmas sweaters they'd bought last year. She grabbed the one on top and unfolded it, holding it up to her chest.

"We're wearing these this year," she said adamantly as she fumbled for the little controller that would turn the dangling, colored bulbs and Rudolph's nose on.

"Of course we are." A goofy grin formed as Tate pulled his out and dragged it over his head. "What do you think?"

They'd gone all out last year and found a couple of rather hideous sweaters in an effort to cheer themselves up. It hadn't worked—the cheering up part—but they'd struck ugly sweater gold. Tate's was eye-catching green with little white snowflakes embroidered all over it and green tinsel draped back and forth from arm to arm. The miniature red and green ornaments that hung from the tinsel jingled when he moved. Hers was red, with Rudolph's face taking up the entire front. A string of lights draped on the antlers, a big red bulb nose, and a green and blue striped scarf dangled down from around his neck.

"I think you look mah-velous, dah-ling," she drawled dramatically as she shoved her arms into hers. "And me?"

"Mah-velous, sweetie," he echoed before walking over to the Christmas tree to plug it in. "Oh, thank God. They all work."

Considering the tree was twelve feet tall—something she had insisted on getting now that they had their new place—they would've been hard-pressed to string it with lights if it hadn't been designed with them already on it.

Reilly chuckled. "Best invention ever."

"The pre-lit tree?" He turned to face her and put a hand on his hip. "I'm not sure I agree."

"Why?" Reilly reached for the other box and opened it to find their ornaments from last year. Her mother had given them the blue and silver ones. As she stared at them now, she wasn't sure that was the theme she wanted to go with this year.

"For starters, I was thinking battery-operated boyfriends might be higher on the list."

She peered up at him and nodded slowly. "You might have a valid point there, Riggs."

"I do, don't I?"

"Speaking of battery-operated boyfriends," she said as she put the lid back on the ornament box and grabbed the small box. "I think—" She laughed. "Oh, damn. Look at this."

Tate strolled to the kitchen, returning with both mugs of hot chocolate. "What is it?"

Reilly lowered to her knees in front of the couch, pulling out envelopes and dropping them onto the coffee table, pausing only long enough to accept one of the cups. Each envelope had a year scrawled across the front in either her neat, curly handwriting or Tate's chicken scratch.

"Are those...?" He moved around and sat on the couch to her left.

"Our hot chocolate wishes. Yeah." Her grin widened as she recalled how they'd sat down every year to write down the one thing they hoped Santa would bring them. It had become a tradition involving massive amounts of hot chocolate and a lot of serious consideration. After all, making a wish was a big deal, right? It had to be perfect.

"Holy shit." Tate grabbed one of the envelopes. "This one's from when we were eleven."

Reilly glanced at the envelope dated 2011 as she sipped her hot chocolate. "I wanted..." She licked the melted marshmallow off her lip. "Probably an iPhone, but I bet I got Monster High dolls that year."

Her parents had worked extra hard to ensure she didn't grow up too fast.

Tate opened the envelope. "Yep. iPhone. Both of us."

She laughed. They'd been best friends since they were in first grade, and for as long as she could remember, they'd wanted the same things for Christmas and birthdays. Mostly. Tate hadn't been on board with the idea of four-inch sparkly heels she'd been eyeing when they were in ninth grade, but he'd been all over the pink tutu she asked for when she was eight.

"What about this one?" Tate asked, flashing the envelope with 2016 written on it.

"No doubt, a truck," she said.

Tate opened it and looked at the card, then laughed before turning it around so she could see it.

"A brand-new Silverado," she read. "I didn't get that, either. But I did have an iPhone by then."

"And 2018?" Tate said, holding up the envelope.

Reilly frowned. "We would've been seniors in high school, so... I don't know. Open it."

Tate opened the flap and pulled out the card. He barked a laugh and turned it so she could read it.

Reilly's cheeks warmed. "For Brady McCord to fall deeply in love with me."

Yeah. She'd pretty much wanted that every year, but that was the first year she'd been brave enough to write it down.

"Here's mine," Tate said, showing her.

"For Donovan Jameson to look at me like a man, not a cute little kid. And kiss me." Reilly scrunched up her nose and did the same thing she did when he first told her he had the hots for her brother. "Eww. Gross. Boy cooties."

Tate laughed, but his eyes softened as he stared at the card. "A ridiculous wish, huh?"

"Not at all," she said with enough conviction she almost believed it.

It wasn't that Reilly didn't think Tate was capable of catching Donovan's eye because she knew he already had, even if he didn't believe it. She'd seen her brother watching him when Donovan didn't think anyone was around to notice. And why wouldn't Donovan be interested in Tate? Tate was mega-cute. She'd always thought so. And back in the fifth grade, she'd thought of him in a slightly different way. The romantic kind of way. Right up until she learned that Tate didn't like her like that. He didn't like *any* girls like that.

Reilly grinned. She still remembered their conversation on her parents' back porch. Reilly'd been upset because the rumor started that she liked Tate, but he didn't like her back. It was then that her very best friend in the whole wide world shared the truth with her. And maybe with himself. He'd been so sweet about it, taking her hand and holding it while he admitted he liked boys, not girls.

It was safe to say she'd fallen in love with him a little more that day, but it was the purest of loves without the complexities of physical attraction to muddy the waters. Reilly had long ago accepted that she would never be what Tate needed in a life partner and vice versa. Needless to say, they'd been even closer since.

But, hello, her big brother Donovan *was* gay, so why in the world wouldn't he want Tate?

Tate was the sweet, boy-next-door kinda cute with his curly blonde hair, big blue eyes, and perfect lips. Not to mention a body even she was envious of. At five-six, Tate considered himself short, which, based on the men in this town, he was. However, his trim, compact body was what athletes everywhere would spend hours and hours attempting to sculpt. He didn't have an ounce of fat on him, and his abs ... washboard was an understatement. And yeah, she was jealous of how easily he'd been able to build that body. No matter how hard she tried, Reilly would never have a sculpted stomach. As far as she was concerned, her hips were too wide, her boobs were too big, and her belly was only flat when she sucked it in. But no amount of sucking it in was going to make her look good in a crop top.

Then again, she could rock a bikini. Or so she'd been told. It was her boobs. Men liked big boobs, and she would be the first to admit hers were rather voluptuous, even if she would've preferred a nice C-cup over the double Ds she'd been gifted with.

But their looks didn't factor into their chances of landing two hot, older men. Her inability to land Brady McCord had nothing to do with her body type and everything to do with the fact that he was turning thirty-nine this year, and she was only twenty-three. There was the same age difference between Donovan and Tate, except Tate's twenty-fourth birthday was coming up in three weeks.

Not that twenty-four was any different than twenty-three. Not when there was a sixteen-year age gap. To add a visual flare, Donovan and Brady were getting their driver's licenses the year Reilly was born. While her mom and dad were rocking her in a cradle, Brady McCord was out racing his friends on the backroads of Coyote Ridge. So it didn't matter that Brady looked at her like he wanted to devour her in one bite. She knew he would never give in to that craving.

Not unless he was enticed to do so.

"You know what?" She turned to look at Tate. "I think we should go for it this year."

Tate wiped marshmallow off his nose, setting his cup on the table. "Go for what?"

She canted her head and waited for him to catch on.

His eyebrows shot up. "You want me to make a play for Donovan?" He snorted. "Your brother's not gonna give me the time of day, and we both know it."

"You won't know if you don't try."

She could tell he was intrigued by the idea, but she knew Tate. He was overly skeptical. Not to mention a little shy.

"Seriously," she said, reaching for the envelope. "Give me a pen."

Tate hopped up from the couch and hurried to the kitchen, rummaging through the junk drawer. He returned with a pen.

Reilly took it and looked at the logo. It was a pen from M-J Architecture & Interiors, the firm her brother and Brady owned. "Apropos."

She grabbed the envelope from 2018 and put a line through the year, then wrote 2023 below it. She turned it around and showed Tate.

"You up for it?"

He stared at the envelope for the longest time.

"Come on, Tate. We've got to grab the bulls by the horns. We're single. They're single."

"There's only one problem with that, sweetie," he said, his expression serious.

"What's that?"

"We're delusional. *They* are not."

Reilly laughed, nearly snorting hot chocolate out of her nose.

"Live a little, Tate."

"And what if they don't go for it?"

"We won't give them a chance to back down. All's fair in love and war, right?"

Tate smirked and rolled his eyes.

She added, "There's no better time than the present."

"You're just a little ball of cliches today, huh?" Tate grumbled, his blue eyes glittering with amusement.

She grinned because she could do this all day. "When life gives you lemons, make lemonade."

"Fine."

"Really?"

"Yeah." His grin widened. "I'm in."

Reilly squealed. "Yay!" She reached for her hot chocolate. "Now let's drink to the best hot chocolate wishes ever!"

He picked up his cup and clinked it against hers before taking a sip.

"*Hwaahh.*" His nose scrunched. "Is this straight liqueur? Jesus."

"Lightweight," she said before taking a generous gulp. Her nostrils flared. He was right. She'd overdone it just a little.

He set his cup down. "You know if we start drinking, we won't get the tree decorated."

She placed her cup on the table and reached for her laptop. "Right. Ornaments. We need new ones."

"Wait. New? Wha—huh? What's wrong with the ones we have?"

"Wrong color."

Tate shook his head as he lifted the lid on the ornament box. "Of course they are."

"I think red and gold will be the theme for this year." She pulled up Amazon's website. "Ooh and look. There's a sale on a fifteen-foot-tall inflatable snowman."

Tate flopped back on the couch. "It's a wonder we ever get anything done."

Two

"WHAT ARE YOU DOIN'?"

Reilly glanced down at her father from her perch on the step ladder she had dragged in from the garage. "Hangin' decorations. What are *you* doin'?"

"Watchin' you string up mistletoe. I thought this was a birthday party."

"It is," she told him as though it made perfect sense to be strategically placing mistletoe throughout her parents' house.

In all fairness, she'd already strung it up in the barn, although she and Tate were going out of their way to avoid it whenever they moved around. She seriously doubted Donovan or Brady would ever wander that way, but in the event they did, they were ready for them. Of course, she was *not* kissing her brother if he happened to be standing beneath it, but he was fair game for Tate.

"And mistletoe, *why*?"

"Because it's festive, Daddy." She started down the ladder and accepted his hand when he reached to help her.

"And you get a kick out of seein' me make out with your mama?"

"Eww. No." She grinned. "But you're welcome."

Owen Jameson shook his head, but he was still smiling. Her father had learned to deal with her craziness. Her family called it an endearing quality, although she knew it mostly annoyed them. Then again, she was the baby, so it was allowed.

Not only was she the youngest of her parents' five children, but she was also the youngest on her level of the family tree. Of all her cousins on her father's side, at twenty-three, Reilly was at the very, very bottom. The closest was Rafe, and he was eight years older than her. Worse than that, her sister was ten years older than her.

A happy accident, her father liked to call her.

While she enjoyed the attention that came from being the youngest of twenty-eight cousins and four siblings, there was also a downside. Like the fact that she was usually the one relegated to the little kid's table at family meals. It also meant she had to work twice as hard to get away with anything in this small town.

It seemed everyone in Coyote Ridge was keeping an eye on her. If she made one misstep, someone was telling either her parents or her oldest brother because Donovan was her only sibling who constantly stuck his nose in her business. Stone didn't live in Coyote Ridge, so she didn't have to worry about him. And Chase, whom everyone called CJ, was too busy to worry about her antics, as he kindly referred to anything she did. Her sister, Chelsea, moved to Dallas last year when she got married, but they talked at least once a week. Chelsea knew all about Reilly's long-running crush on Donovan's best friend, as well as most of her stunts even before she pulled them.

What was awesome about it was Reilly didn't care that she was surrounded by all those tattletales. Sure, it had been a pain in her behind growing up, having to deal with all the overprotective people keeping a close eye on everything she did. But it was also cool in the sense that she'd never been without someone around to keep her company.

Of course, now that she was a grown woman, dodging all those well-meaning, overprotective family members required time management. Unfortunately, time was often something she was lacking, so she ended up walking into her own trap.

But not today.

Up to this point, she'd made absolutely no traction on her pact with Tate. No matter how hard she tried, she couldn't pin Brady down. According to her mother, Brady and Donovan were buried in work, finishing up one of the biggest projects their firm had undertaken since they started it nearly a decade ago. Because of that, Reilly wasn't running into Brady as much as she usually did.

But today, he would be right where she wanted him, and she intended to be ready.

"There's a car out front," her mother called from where she was sitting at the dining room table with Aunt Lorrie and Uncle Curtis.

Reilly turned and watched her dad move to the living room window, waiting not-so-patiently for him to broadcast who it was.

"It's Chelsea," he announced.

Reilly squealed and took off out the front door, racing to her sister's car. "You're here!"

"I'm here," Chelsea said as she slowly eased out of the car, her hand protectively covering her pregnant belly.

"Hi, Paul," Reilly greeted her brother-in-law.

"Rye. How's it goin'?"

"It's goin'," she said, looping her arm through one of Chelsea's while Paul took her other hand.

"It hasn't rained in a few days, but Dad made sure there's no ice just in case," Reilly told her sister.

Plus, it was above freezing, but Reilly didn't feel the need to tack that on. She didn't want Mother Nature to overhear and think that was her way of summoning some tragic ice storm like they'd seen in the past. Snow was never a problem around here, but the ice could be brutal.

"Y'all realize I'm only six months pregnant, right? I'm quite capable of maintaining my balance at this point."

"Sure you are," Paul said at the same time Reilly said, "Keep tellin' yourself that."

Reilly figured she didn't need to remind Chelsea just how clumsy she was. And that was when there wasn't the equivalent of a basketball blocking her view of her feet.

"Hi, Daddy," Chelsea greeted their father when they made it up to the porch.

"Hi, sugar." He leaned in and kissed her, then stepped out of the way.

"Okay, you two, let me go. I've got to pee," Chelsea said, pulling away.

Reilly released her sister, and before she could ask her father when Stone would arrive, she heard the sound of tires crunching on gravel behind her. She spun around to see Stone's big F350 making its way up the driveway.

She waited until he parked, then skipped down the steps and out to the driver's side of the truck.

Her brother got out, but not before grabbing his cowboy hat and setting it on his head.

"Hey, pipsqueak," he greeted, accepting her hug when she threw her arms around him. "How's it hangin'?"

"Low and to the left," she deadpanned.

He came up short and stared at her before barking a laugh. "You know what that means, right?"

"Of course I do. I've got three big brothers. Where do you think I learned it?"

"We ruined you, kid."

"You totally did," she told him, putting her arm around his waist when he put his around her shoulder and steered her toward the house. "How long are you gonna be in town?"

"I gotta head back to Houston tonight."

"Aw, man."

"I know, kid. But I promise I'll make it up to you on your birthday."

Her birthday wasn't until February, but she knew Stone would stand by his promise. He was busy, so she understood he couldn't make his way up here as often as he would've liked. He worked on a ranch down in Houston where they raised bulls specifically bred to compete in PBR rodeos. Stone didn't like to be away from it for too long.

"Is CJ or D here?" Stone asked when they reached the porch.

"CJ should be here any minute," she told him. "And we gave Donovan and Brady a delayed time."

"And Tate?"

"He's at home," she said, gesturing toward the barn at the back of the property.

"You two get that place finished yet?"

"We did. Back in August."

"How're you likin' it?"

"It's drafty," she said honestly. "But don't tell Mama I said that."

Reilly had harped on her mother and father for a solid year, begging them to let her convert the barn into a house. They'd never used it for anything other than an extra garage back when her brothers and sisters lived there. She was constantly showing them pictures of fancy barndominiums that had become all the rage around these parts. When they finally relented, it was only with the condition that Donovan and Brady be responsible for the architectural changes. It turned out even better than Reilly expected, with the only downside being the ceiling was so tall it was nearly impossible to regulate the temperature in the common areas.

Stone winked. "Your secret's safe with me, kid."

"You should come by before you leave. I'll give you the nickel tour."

"Count on it," he said before he released her to greet their father with a back-slapping hug. "Hey, old man."

Reilly was about to walk inside when she heard tires on gravel again. She turned, expecting to see CJ pulling in, but the car that navigated the pot-holed driveway did not belong to anyone in her family.

"Who's that?" Stone asked, coming to stand beside her.

"Someone who's not invited," she said, glaring as the car passed the main house and headed for the barn. "I'll be back in a minute. I've got to go rip Tate a new one."

TATE RIGGS SAT ON THE BARSTOOL AND stared at the email he'd received an hour ago. It was from his mother. Against his better judgment, he'd reached out to her a few weeks ago to see how she was doing. Since she never answered her phone and refused to respond to his text messages, he'd resorted to sending an email.

He should've known better. In simple terms, his mother had nothing to say to him because he'd chosen the life he wanted, and she had no place in it.

That was the word she'd always used. Chosen. According to her, Tate had *chosen* to be gay, and therefore, he'd outright defied her wishes. She couldn't tolerate the idea of it and had decided to shut him out of her life when he was seventeen. She'd kicked him out of her house and told him he could only come back when he came to his senses.

Her response was: *if you haven't accepted that you're living a life of sin, I don't see any room in my life for you.*

No doubt he had expected her to say that, but there had been a bit of hope glimmering for a while. Those words effectively doused that tiny flame.

Tate exhaled with a sigh. "I guess the day can't get much worse."

As soon as the words were out of his mouth, Tate heard the sound of a car door shut. He peered over his shoulder at the windows overlooking the spot they used for parking at the side entrance.

"What the fuck?"

He got to his feet, his eyebrows peeled back as he stared at the black Hyundai. Only one person he knew drove that kind of car.

"Spoke too soon," he muttered, closing the lid on his laptop, intending to head his visitor off at the pass.

Tate started to open the door because there was no way in hell he was letting that man in his house, and that was when he saw Reilly racing from the main house.

He would've laughed because Reilly insisted she would only run if there was an apocalypse and zombies were after her—her idea of the worst thing that could happen. Which meant she considered this visitor to be the equivalent of a doomsday event.

He reached for the doorknob to interrupt, but it didn't open when he pulled. Tate jerked the handle as though that would help but realized it was locked at the top. He reached for the sliding pin on the doorjamb, trying to wiggle it loose, but it was stuck.

"Shit." He stared in horror as Reilly's mouth opened. "Shit, shit, shit."

"What the fuck are you doin' here?" she shouted at the visitor before Tate could get outside.

"I came to see Tate. You got a problem with that?"

"A big one," she said, stopping right in front of him and planting her hands on her hips. "Yeah."

Again, Tate wanted to laugh because she was huffing like a freight train.

"Good thing he doesn't answer to you."

Tate finally got the pin free and jerked the door open. He stepped out onto the extra-wide porch that ran the length of the barn on one side. "It's okay, Reilly."

She cocked her head to the side and gave him the *are you fucking kidding me?* expression she was known for.

"What are you doin' here?" Tate asked Ben.

Ben was looking at the house. "You live in a barn?"

Tate pretended not to notice the way he spat the last word.

"What do you need, Ben?"

"I need her not to attack me from behind," he said, his full attention on Reilly.

"Trust me, I'll attack from the front, so you know I'm comin'," Reilly hissed.

"Rye." Tate moved closer to the steps. "It's cool."

Apparently, his definition of *cool* and her definition clashed because she glared at him.

His ex-boyfriend's gaze shifted back to him, and his chin tilted up as though he'd won that round. Ben was too stupid to realize he would never win against Reilly. She was fiercely loyal and hated Ben because of the hell he'd put Tate through.

Ben slipped his hands into the pockets of his camel-colored, double-breasted, knee-length overcoat. At one point in time, Tate had found the man ridiculously appealing. Now he merely found him ridiculous. Especially since he'd paired that pretentious coat with a chocolate brown turtleneck sweater and tan, slim-fit chinos. If Tate had to guess, he'd selected the outfit directly from the Macy's website from the "wear it with" section.

Ben met Tate's gaze. "Do you think we could go inside?"

The snarl on Ben's lip said he didn't really trust to go inside, worried he might find himself knee-deep in horseshit.

The good news was, the only horseshit around there was anything that came out of Ben's lying, cheating mouth.

"Tate Bellamy Riggs," Reilly called from behind Ben's car.

He waved her off. "It's okay, sweetie."

It was obvious she didn't believe him, but he appreciated that she turned and headed back to the main house. Not without turning back around at least half a dozen times in the process, though.

Tate turned his attention to Ben. "Why're you here?"

"It's your birthday," Ben said, plastering one of his sunny smiles on his pretty face.

"Technically, not until Monday," Tate countered.

"I know, but you know how it is when you work a nine-to-five."

Actually, Tate didn't know. This was a point of contention between him and Ben during the year they'd dated. As an EMT, Tate's schedule fluctuated, but for the most part, he worked either twelve or twenty-four-hour shifts three days a week. Ben had hated that Tate wasn't around when he expected him to be. Or at least that was what Ben told him when Tate found out the guy was cheating on him.

Ben pulled his hands free of his pockets and began fidgeting with the fingers of his leather gloves. No doubt, he wanted Tate to see them because, for Ben, the clothes made the man, and if he wasn't showing off every accessory, he wasn't doing his job.

Considering it was a mild day, there was a good chance Ben was sweating like a whore in church but doing his best to pretend otherwise.

"I was thinking maybe I could take you to dinner tonight," Ben offered.

"I've got plans."

"With?"

"It doesn't matter."

"Ah." Ben nodded his head slowly. "Spending it with Reilly, huh? You know, she's probably part of why you can't keep a boyfriend."

Tate bit his tongue, refusing to reduce himself to Ben's level. The reason he couldn't keep a boyfriend was because the last one he'd had was a lying, cheating whore. But he was past reminding Ben of that fact. No matter what, Ben refused to believe he was at fault for their breakup nearly eight months ago.

"How did you find out where I live?" Tate asked, realizing when they'd last been together, Tate hadn't lived here.

"The benefits of a backward, redneck town," Ben said, and it was not meant as a compliment. "People don't value privacy."

Great.

"Well," Ben said dramatically, shifting so his coat flared around his knees. "I guess I should go."

When he looked back, Tate knew he was waiting for an invitation to whatever Tate's plans were for the evening. He wasn't getting one.

Tate released a pent-up breath when Ben started down the porch steps.

"I'd like to catch up, Tate. Maybe next weekend?"

"Yeah, maybe," he said merely to get Ben to keep walking. He had no desire to spend time in Ben's company, but he also wasn't looking to argue with the man.

"Perfect," Ben said, grinning as though Tate had agreed. "I saw a sign for a festival in town. Are you planning to go to it?"

"I go every year," he reminded Ben. Not that he needed the reminder. Last year, they'd argued when Tate insisted on going with Reilly. Ben had tagged along and bitched the entire night.

"Then it's a date," Ben said before turning toward his car.

"It's not a date," Tate called out.

Ben flashed another pearly white smile. "Sure it is. You just need to admit you're not over me yet."

Tate rolled his eyes and went back inside. Oh, he was definitely over him, all right. Even if he weren't, Tate wouldn't touch that man with a ten-foot pole. Like he said, lying, cheating whore.

He was only inside for about three minutes before the door opened, and Reilly stomped inside, her boots knocking on the concrete floor. She had to have been watching from her parents' house.

"Why was he here?" she asked, her tone civil, although he knew she had to work hard to mask her anger.

"He wanted to take me out for my birthday."

She stared at him. Tate could practically see all the things she wanted to say flashing in her eyes. She hated Ben. Maybe even more than Tate did, and that was saying something.

"I told him no," he assured her.

"Good." She ran her hands down the front of her sweater. "That's good."

Tate grinned. "I love you, you know that?"

She smiled. "I do know. I love you, too. Which is why I'm willin' to stomp his ass into dust for you."

She wasn't kidding. Reilly had thrown more than one punch in his honor over the years. Granted, he hadn't needed her to since high school, but she always ensured he knew she was still ready to go to bat for him. He loved her for that. She was his sister in all ways that mattered. Well, except he had the hots for her brother, so he didn't think of her like a sister. It was too creepy to consider.

"You about ready?" she asked, gesturing toward his legs.

Tate glanced down. "You have a problem with what I'm wearin'?"

"I don't know. You want Donovan to see you in your Snoopy pajamas?"

"That's fair," he said, laughing. "I was about to shower when Ben showed up."

Reilly looked at her watch. "You better hurry."

"You said two, right?"

"Yes."

"I've got half an hour. And a one-minute commute. I promise I'll be there on time."

"You better." She spun around to leave but detoured to the kitchen island. She snatched one of his chocolate croissants and raised it high as she marched toward the door.

"Hey! Your mom made those for me!"

"It's payback for makin' me look at that lyin', cheatin' whore on a Saturday."

"I didn't invite him!" Tate shouted, although she was already outside.

Reilly kept walking and threw up her other hand in a gesture that said, *what can you do?*

Tate grinned. Yeah. She made his life interesting.

Three

Brady McCord arrived at the Jamesons' house exactly at two-thirty, as he was told to do.

It didn't take a rocket scientist to figure out it was a birthday party. They held one every year for him, Donovan, and Tate since their birthdays were all within a few days of each other. Even growing up, Brady had always shared his birthday celebration with Donovan because their mothers had been best friends since they were kids. The fact Brady was born one day after Donovan was merely a coincidence but something that thrilled both of their mothers.

From his first memories, Brady had spent most of his time at the Jamesons' house. Since his father—nothing more than a sperm donor, really—left before Brady was born, his mom had raised him on his own with help from her friends. And when his mother died last year, just two weeks before Christmas after a long bout with cancer, Brady had leaned on the Jamesons then, too.

The holiday hadn't been the same without his mother, that was for sure. And he wasn't the only one impacted by the loss. Deborah Jameson had been brokenhearted, but she'd kept it together for him. And for Reilly. Brady knew Reilly had felt helpless because she'd considered Eve her second mom. Brady hadn't known how to console her then, so he'd kept his distance, hoping her parents would help her through it.

Needless to say, there hadn't been much to celebrate last year. They had understood when he told them he didn't want to celebrate his birthday because he'd been making funeral arrangements for his mother. In fact, Deborah had helped him through the entire ordeal, never leaving his side.

While they'd all gone through a long period of mourning during the months that followed, this year, they'd decided to go with tradition because that was what his mother would've wanted. Brady wasn't thrilled with celebrating this year, but he knew the Jamesons needed this as much as he did, so here he was.

As he got out of his SUV, he waited for Donovan to pull up beside him and park. They'd been finishing up some work at the office that morning, working right up until they risked being late for their own party. Although Donovan would've gladly been late, Brady didn't do tardy well.

"You up for gettin' a beer later?" Donovan asked when he came around the front of his truck.

"I don't need a babysitter, D."

"Maybe I do."

Brady laughed. He appreciated his best friend's desire to keep him company. For the past year, Donovan had been keeping close tabs on him. Brady had been close to his mother, and yes, he missed her terribly. What most people didn't understand, though, was that Brady had hated seeing her in so much pain for the last few months of her life. So his reflections were bittersweet. He was moving forward exactly as he'd promised his mother he would do.

"Fair warnin'," Owen Jameson said when he walked out onto the porch. "Reilly's been hangin' mistletoe all mornin'."

"Noted," Donovan said, hugging his dad.

Brady waited his turn, then did the same before entering the house.

"Happy Birthday!" everyone shouted in unison, smiling like idiots as they stood shoulder to shoulder as though they'd been waiting for the guests of honor to arrive.

Stone looked at Reilly. "We're good, right? That's it?"

Reilly nodded. "I'm good if you are."

CJ nodded. "Cool."

Before Brady could say anything, everyone scattered. Donovan's parents, Owen and Deborah, took seats on the couch. Reilly, Chelsea, and Chelsea's husband went to the dining room and started playing cards. Donovan's aunt and uncle, Lorrie and Curtis, sat on the loveseat and turned their attention to the television while his uncle Mitch and aunt Janice perched on the ends of the couch. Tate—who was also a guest of honor—flopped into Owen's recliner and kicked his feet up. Stone and CJ disappeared toward the kitchen.

"Well, I guess that's it then," Donovan said, clapping Brady on the shoulder and turning back to the door.

"I think I'll grab that beer with you," he told Donovan.

"Get your butts in here," Deborah called as she got to her feet, smiling merrily. "Come here and give me hugs."

"Just out of curiosity, how many years in a row do you plan to do that?" Donovan asked his mother.

"As many as we want," she said with a lift of her chin before she hugged them both. "Are you hungry?"

"I could eat," Brady told her.

He was as at home at the Jamesons as any of their children. He'd spent a good portion of his life here, so he didn't consider himself a guest so much as family. He couldn't count how many dishes he'd cleaned over the years or how many bags of trash he'd taken out. Owen and Deborah treated him like one of their own.

"Beer?" Owen offered when he joined them in the kitchen.

"Sure, thanks."

Owen grabbed two bottles from the refrigerator, then used one to point toward the ceiling. Brady looked up in time to see a sprig of mistletoe dangling just a few feet to his right. Brady skimmed the rest of the ceiling and grinned. Reilly had certainly outdone herself. You could hardly move ten feet in any direction before encountering another.

Brady took the mistletoe as a sign, which he figured was Reilly's intention. For years, he'd endured Donovan's baby sister flirting ruthlessly with him. And fine, maybe *endured* wasn't quite the right word. He'd been flattered. And in recent years, flattered had shifted to interested. Not that he was willing to admit to that. Dating his best friend's little sister was a surefire way of ensuring his friendship with Donovan died a slow, agonizing death. Brady wasn't willing to risk that.

21

"It was Tate's turn to pick the food," CJ noted.

"Tacos?" Donovan and Brady asked at the same time.

The kid loved Deborah's taco salad, and since the rest of them usually turned their noses up at anything with leafy greens in it, they got tacos instead.

"You two take a seat," Deborah said. "I'll make your plates and bring 'em to you."

Brady followed Donovan into the formal dining room at the front of the house, both of them careful to skirt two more sprigs of mistletoe dangling overhead.

When he walked into the dining room, he saw Reilly looking at the ceiling, likely checking to see if one of them got stuck in her trap. When she realized they hadn't, her gaze shifted to him.

Like every time she looked at him, he was momentarily speechless. In all fairness, that hadn't happened until recently. Last year, sometime, he figured. Brady didn't know what had caused the shift, allowing him to see her as a woman and not a kid who was sixteen years younger than him, but it had happened all the same.

Not that it mattered. Reilly was Donovan's baby sister, and therefore, she was completely off-limits. The age gap only helped to keep him from wanting something he could never have.

"Who's winnin'?" Donovan asked as he dropped into the seat beside Reilly.

"Me," Reilly said as Chelsea and her husband, Paul, pointed at her.

"Are they lettin' you win?"

"Never," Chelsea said at the same time Reilly said, "Don't underestimate my ability, D. I'll kick your ass at poker any day of the week."

"We're playin' rummy," Chelsea noted.

Reilly grinned. "Oh. Well, I'm even better than I thought."

Brady couldn't help but laugh. The woman was absolutely fucking adorable, and he wasn't the only one who thought so. Her entire family adored her. Hell, everyone who knew her did. She always had a sassy quip ready, and she rarely took life too seriously. He appreciated that about her. It made him feel young simply being in her presence.

Deborah came in a minute later, sliding plates in front of them.

"Tate! Food's ready!" Reilly shouted.

Tate strolled in with a grin as he stared at the enormous tortilla shell bowl of lettuce piled high with ground beef, refried beans, shredded cheese, and diced tomatoes. All drenched in Tate's favorite: jalapeño ranch dressing.

"Mama, can I have salad, too?" Reilly asked, eyeballing Tate's food.

When she reached to dip her finger in his dressing, Tate poked her with his fork.

"You already stole my croissant."

"You shouldn't let that douchebag come to our house," she retorted, her voice low.

"What douchebag are we talkin' about?" Chelsea asked, glancing between them.

Everyone chimed in at the same time with, "Ben."

Tate's gaze slid from one face to the next, and Brady noticed his cheeks turning pink.

Donovan leaned around Reilly to pin Tate with a glare. "Why's he comin' around?"

Tate sighed. "Thanks, Rye."

"No problem."

"He's not comin' around," Tate replied, not looking at Donovan. "He showed up unannounced. Wanted to take me out for my birthday."

Donovan wasn't finished glaring at him.

Brady sat back, amused as always that Donovan was as protective of Tate as he was of Reilly. Had been the case for years. At least from the time Tate moved into the Jamesons' house after his mother kicked him out when he was seventeen.

"Don't worry," Tate added. "Reilly threatened to kick his ass."

"I'll do it, too. And twice on Sunday," she said, looking down at her cards.

Brady loved how fiercely loyal and protective she was.

"And I'll help," Donovan grumbled, rubbing his knuckles on Reilly's head. "Can't let you have all the fun."

"Reilly's a badass," Stone joked as he pulled up a chair at the table. "But someone might wanna warn him D's gunnin' for him."

Brady was looking at Reilly, so he noticed her little crooked smirk and the way her eyebrow quirked. It was one of her many tells. Or, more accurately, a sign that she was up to something.

And that was never good.

He received confirmation a second later when she looked at him and winked.

DONOVAN JAMESON SAT BACK IN HIS DAD'S recliner and listened to the ruckus echoing through his parents' house. It had been like this since he walked in nearly three hours ago. Through the meal, then as they opened their gifts, and finally when they lit the candles on all three cakes—a tradition his mother insisted on—and sang their off-key rendition of Happy Birthday.

The only difference between then and now was that his aunts and uncles had left. Everyone else was still there, just hanging out.

Reilly and Chelsea were in the living room, talking under their breaths. If he had to guess, the topic of their conversation was Brady, although Reilly tried to pretend she didn't have a thing for him. Donovan knew better. He also knew his best friend had eyes for his little sister. Donovan got the feeling Brady was sticking by the bro code: *best friends don't date best friend's little sister.* Perhaps he should've been more worried about Brady and Reilly ending up together, but to be fair, Donovan didn't know a better man for his sister. Brady was a stand-up guy, loyal and honest. Why wouldn't Donovan want that for her?

Approving or not, he wasn't going to give them a nudge. Either they would figure it out, or they wouldn't. Not his problem.

Mom and Dad were talking to Stone, getting the lowdown on all things cowboy. He was the one they saw the least, even though they tried to make it to Houston every couple of months for a weekend. Donovan saw him even less than that, but they kept in touch by phone.

Then there was CJ. He'd been texting on his phone since he got there. If Donovan had ten guesses who he was chatting with, every single one would be the same: Jamie Collier. CJ'd had a thing for her for quite some time now. Since they were texting back and forth, he had to think they'd progressed from the point where CJ simply spent his Saturday nights staring at her across the bar.

Paul, Brady, and Tate were still at the dining room table talking about sports. He found it amusing since Tate wasn't much of a football fan, yet he could hold his own in a conversation. Donovan could credit Reilly for that. She was a fanatic—a Dallas Cowboys fan through and through—and through the years, she'd imparted her best friend with her knowledge.

The kicker was Donovan had never cared whether or not Tate was up to speed on stats or upcoming games. He'd always considered Tate to be an extension of Reilly. When Reilly and Tate were young, Donovan had seen him as another member of the family. One who was always around.

But Donovan had never seen him as a kid brother. No. They'd never developed that sort of bond. And after their conversation back when Tate turned seventeen, Donovan started seeing him in an entirely different light—the kind that shone with keen interest and, yes, an underlying physical attraction.

There was something about Tate Riggs that called to something deep inside Donovan. Something he'd never felt with anyone else. For years, he'd chalked it up to a distorted sense of family obligation. Or that was what he tried to tell himself, anyway. Truth was, Donovan was attracted to him. Not only physically but on a deeper level. He admired Tate. Perhaps it was Tate's ability to stand up for himself or how he accepted that other people wouldn't change, no matter how much you wished they would. Tate was a realist.

A very sweet, very cute one.

Whatever the reason for Donovan's recent and inappropriate interest in the kid, Donovan couldn't help himself. On top of that, he didn't understand it. Then again, he wasn't trying to. The last thing Donovan needed was to get mixed up with a guy who didn't understand the meaning of a one-night stand. For as long as Donovan had known Tate to be interested in someone, he'd been in one relationship after another, most at least semi-serious. Donovan preferred the opposite. But what did he know? His usual type was the exact opposite of Tate Riggs, yet he still found himself thinking about the guy far more often than he should.

As though he could sense Donovan thinking about him, Tate's eyes cut to him. It was only a brief look, but it was enough to remind Donovan there were people around. People who noticed shit he didn't want them to notice.

"Anyone want another beer?" Donovan asked as he pushed to his feet and headed for the kitchen, taking the route through the living room so he didn't risk catching anyone's eye.

"I'll take one," his father said.

"None for me. I'm headin' out in a couple of minutes," Stone told him, reaching out to stop Donovan before he could pass by. "Reilly showed me the barn. Y'all did a phenomenal job."

"Thanks."

Stone lightly punched his shoulder. "It was good to see you."

"Yeah, you too." Donovan hugged him. "Don't be a stranger. And if you're needin' company down there, just holler. I'm sure I can round up a couple of assholes and send 'em your way."

Stone laughed. "You and Brady are welcome anytime."

"Hey!" Brady hollered from the dining room. "I heard that."

Donovan laughed and bumped Stone's shoulder. "Be careful on your way home."

"Always."

"I'll take a beer," Brady shouted. "Since you're talkin' shit."

With a smile on his face, Donovan headed to the kitchen. He grabbed two beers from the fridge, popped the tops with the opener, carried one to his father, the other to Brady, and returned to the kitchen to get one for himself.

Listening to Stone say his goodbyes, Donovan moved to the back door. He stared at the five acres of dead grass behind his parents' house. They'd only fenced in a small portion. Big enough for a swimming pool suitable for a house full of kids and an outdoor kitchen they used more often than the one inside.

He took a sip of his beer and looked at the barn. He smiled. It looked so much different than it had this time last year. A year ago, they'd been four months into the significant renovation and had finally completed shoring up the walls and ceiling and cutting out all the dead, rotted wood. Donovan and Brady had put their heads together and come up with what turned out to be Reilly and Tate's dream house. Or so they claimed. Being that it was practically in his parents' backyard, Donovan didn't see it as a forever home for either of them, but he was glad they liked it.

With a grin, he headed back to join the football conversation, slipping down the hallway that ran from the kitchen to the dining room when he nearly ran Tate over. In his defense, no one usually used that hallway, opting to come in through the living room.

"A little crowded in here, huh?" Donovan said, sidestepping Tate.

Tate's gaze shot up to the ceiling, then back to Donovan's face, eyes wide.

Donovan looked up and realized he was standing underneath the mistletoe.

Of course he was.

Because that was the way his luck was going these days. He wouldn't call it bad luck. More like his timing was off on nearly everything.

"It's cool," Tate said, turning to move past Donovan in the narrow hallway. "We'll pretend it didn't happen."

"If that's the way you wanna play it."

Tate stopped moving, and now they were standing nearly toe to toe. Donovan was a full head taller than Tate, and at this proximity, Tate had to tilt his head back to look at him.

That shouldn't have turned Donovan on so damn much, but his dick found it incredibly appealing.

He mentally cut himself off from any more beer because, clearly, he'd had more than he thought.

What the hell was he thinking? Taunting Tate? Had he lost his mind completely?

Donovan skimmed Tate's face, his gaze lingering on those perfect fucking lips. What the hell. He was already knee-deep. He might as well go all in since it required a shovel to dig out of already.

Donovan put his free hand on the wall behind Tate and leaned in. "You think you can handle me, little boy?"

Tate swallowed, but there was a flash of something in his big blue eyes. Whatever it was, it turned Donovan on even more.

He really needed to get laid. It had been far too long since he'd had the time to pound himself into some willing stranger. Way too damn long; otherwise, he damn sure wouldn't have been entertaining the idea of bending Tate over and—

Donovan shook off the thought but held his ground with Tate.

"It's your game," Donovan told him. "I know how my sister's mind works. If I had to guess, this was her plan."

Tate's gaze dropped to Donovan's mouth. "Why couldn't it be my plan?"

"Was it?"

Tate looked him in the eye. "Maybe."

The smart thing to do would've been to laugh it off, but Donovan found himself transfixed by the much younger man. He thought of all the ways he could corrupt that sweet, innocent body.

Fuck.

"I'll give you till three, then I'll let you off the hook," Donovan told him. "Three ... two..."

Before he could purse his lips to say one, Tate grabbed him by the back of the neck and pulled him in. Tate's warm breath fanned his mouth for a fraction of a second before the kid finally closed the gap, kissing him.

Donovan meant to pull back and smile, to chalk it up to tradition or whatnot, but he found himself stepping closer, angling his head and licking Tate's lower lip. It must have surprised Tate because his lips parted, and Donovan used the opportunity to slide his tongue into Tate's mouth.

Oh, fuck. This was wrong on so many levels, but Donovan didn't give a shit. Not in the moment, not with Tate's tongue gliding against his. The guy's hesitance was so fucking sexy it made Donovan's dick throb.

A soft moan escaped Tate, and that was nearly all she wrote. By sheer force of will, Donovan kept his hand on the wall and the other firmly around his beer bottle. If he had even one free, he would've grabbed Tate, tossed him over his shoulder, and found somewhere private so he could—

He cut off the thought before the mental image could form. His memories of this kiss were going to be bad enough.

Damn that mistletoe.

"Fuck," he hissed, pulling back only slightly. "You're a temptation I damn sure don't need, little boy."

Tate sucked in a sharp breath, and Donovan locked his restraint back in place, standing tall and smiling. He managed to keep his lips tightly shut as he headed for the dining room to join Brady and Paul.

As he took his seat, he glanced down the hall to find that Tate was gone.

He hated that he was disappointed.

Four

One week later, Saturday, December 23rd

"WHERE'S DONOVAN?" BRADY ASKED WHEN HE STROLLED into the small-town general store.

"Well, merry, happy Chrismukkah to you, too," Reilly greeted, her tone chipper.

As adorable as he found this woman, he'd spent far too much time this past week thinking about her. The only way he was going to move past this absurd infatuation was to spend as little time alone in her company as he possibly could. Coming in here now was a risk, but Donovan had asked him to meet him here rather than drive into Austin so they could sign some papers for a project they were starting next week.

"Where is he, Reilly?"

She flashed a smile but paid him no attention otherwise. "Maybe you misplaced him. Did you look under the tree?"

It took tremendous effort … no, make that *astronomical* effort not to throttle the woman standing across from him.

Not that he would actually throttle her. He wanted to. No, that wasn't true. What he wanted to do was paddle her … Brady tilted his head to the side and admired her impressive ass as she bent over to put a new box of Kit Kats on one of the lower shelves.

Fuck.

He was pretty sure Reilly wore those ass-hugging jeans simply to drive him fucking crazy. Him and every other man she encountered. It fucking worked. Too damn well. The woman had a body made for sin, and although he would never cross that line, he wasn't immune to her. He wished he was. Hell, if they offered a vaccine, he would gladly get it every year simply so he didn't endure moments like this one.

"See somethin' you like?" Reilly taunted, and he realized she'd caught him staring.

Standing tall, Brady exhaled heavily and focused on the reason he'd come in here in the first place.

Deep breath in.

Long breath out.

No sense getting all worked up first thing in the morning.

He glanced around, trying to find the source of the overwhelming cinnamon smell. He noticed a small box of pinecones in a box on the counter.

Brady managed another round of breathing in and out before he chanced another glance at Reilly.

"Can you at least tell me when he'll be back?" he asked, proud of himself for keeping his tone civil.

It wasn't easy. Not when the sexiest brunette in all of Coyote Ridge made it her mission to rile him whenever he saw her.

It'd been that way since… Shit, it was too many years to count. If he did the math, he figured it was going on a decade, at least. In the beginning, it had been harmless flirting. When Reilly was sixteen, he rarely saw her, so he didn't have to worry about it much. Then she turned eighteen and graduated from high school, and he seemed to see her everywhere.

But this past week… Brady was pretty sure she was purposely turning up everywhere he was. Every time he turned around, there she was, tormenting him with something he couldn't have.

It wasn't illegal, and no, they weren't related, but they might as well be since Reilly's older brother, Donovan, just so happened to be Brady's best friend. Since the third grade. And everyone knew that messing with your best friend's little sister was a code you simply didn't break.

Only Reilly didn't seem to be aware of that code. She was set on turning his head, and when she wasn't trying to do that, she was intent on giving him shit if he so much as looked at her.

Reilly stood up and turned toward him, placing her hands on her hips. "You know, they make this thing…" Her lips twisted, and she held up a finger. "Actually, hold on. I know how to fix this."

She sauntered over to the register counter, her denim-clad ass swaying in a way no sane man could resist, still holding her finger up in that all too familiar gesture of *hold on a minute.*

Brady knew he shouldn't, but he waited. Whatever she was about to do was going to frustrate him to no end. Of that, he had no doubt.

He couldn't see what she retrieved from under the counter, but when she came over to where he was standing, she was smiling, her light green eyes glittering with amusement.

"There's this thing." She opened her palm and revealed her cell phone. "It's called a phone." She waggled the phone. "This particular kind is one you can take *wherever* you go." She tapped the screen and then held it up to his face. "You use it to—"

"Smartass," Brady growled as he grabbed for her.

Reilly laughed, that husky voice of hers echoing off the ceiling tiles as she turned to run. She wasn't fast enough, and he wrapped his arm around her waist, stopping her from getting away. Brady pulled her in tight and held her against him while she laughed and snorted, writhing in his arms in her attempt to break free.

He held on for several seconds, then realized what he was doing. Unfortunately, his brain realized it seconds after the rest of his body did, and there was no way to hide his physical reaction to her nearness. His cock was rubbing against her delectable ass, pressing insistently against the zipper of his jeans, broadcasting his undeniable attraction to this woman.

"Is that a cell phone in your pocket, Mr. McCord?" she teased. "Or are you *really* happy to see me?"

Brady released her and backed away, focusing on the breathing techniques that had always helped in stressful situations. And despite his better judgment, this was a stressful situation—possibly the most stressful he'd had in a long damn time.

The bells over the door jingled, and he knew without turning who it was. There was only one person it could be because that was the way this day was going for Brady.

"Hey, man. I was lookin' for you," Donovan said.

Brady glanced over his shoulder and jerked his chin in a silent greeting. He couldn't turn around for obvious reasons. The last thing he needed was for Donovan to kick him in the teeth because he sported a hard-on the size of Texas in Reilly's presence.

Donovan walked into the store, his forehead creased as he assessed the situation.

Brady started doing algebra in his head to wrangle his damn dick into submission. *Two times two is four. Four times four is sixteen. Sixteen times sixteen is two fifty-six. Two fifty-six times—*

"Hey, look," Reilly sing-songed. "There he is now. You're right. He *wasn't* under the tree." She threw up her hands. "Who knew?"

"What's goin' on?" Donovan asked, glancing between the two of them.

Brady was hoping Reilly would explain that he'd come in looking for Donovan so he didn't think Brady was hanging around for the hell of it, but she hurried off to the back of the store, leaving him to deal with her overprotective, clearly not-happy brother.

Granted, Donovan was the reason Brady was there, so technically, the guy had no reason to be unhappy with him. Right?

Right.

Donovan leaned to the side, watching his sister scurry off. When he peered back at him, Brady had the ridiculous urge to assure him that nothing was going on between him and Reilly.

There wasn't.

Then again, for as long as Brady could remember, he wished there was.

Okay, that wasn't true. It hadn't been all that long. A year or so. Maybe two. Fine. It was more like three, but it hadn't been longer than that. That was a fact since Brady had been married before then, so he couldn't have been interested in his best friend's little sister.

Not that any of it mattered. Considering Reilly Jameson was sixteen years younger than Brady, he had absolutely no business wanting her at all. Ever. She was far too young for the likes of him. Young and uncorrupted, unlike Brady.

"Do you have the papers?" Brady asked when his dick began to simmer down.

"I stopped by to pick them up, but they weren't open. I'll try again in a couple of hours."

Brady nodded.

"You wanna grab some lunch or somethin'?" Donovan asked, moving toward the register.

Brady stared at him, trying to remember why the hell he'd come here in the first place.

Thankfully, the door swung open, the bells jingling merrily to announce a customer.

OH, MAN.

Oh man, oh man, oh man.

Reilly stood in the small stock room at the back of the store, her palms flat on the wall as she tried to catch her breath. Her smile was so wide her cheeks hurt and her breaths were sawing in and out of her lungs.

Her body tingled. It actually freaking tingled from Brady's touch. Even now, when he wasn't touching her, she could feel the heat of him, the solid steel of his body as he held her close. And she couldn't forget that unmistakable bulge in his pants. The one that had been pressed against her ass only a few moments ago.

Reilly: 1.

Brady McCord: 0.

She shook her head to dislodge the ridiculousness of keeping score, but her smile never faded. As much as she wished his touch had been intentional, she knew better. However, that didn't mean his reaction had been accidental. Oh, no. She knew without a doubt that Brady McCord wanted her. He simply refused to give in to his baser urges. But she was working on him.

It was taking longer than she'd hoped. If she didn't know better, she would think Brady was onto her plan to seduce him before Christmas. She'd spent every available minute this past week attempting to stage an accidental run-in with the man. She'd failed miserably.

Then suddenly, there he was, standing in the store looking like sin on a stick. She would've given up days ago if she knew she simply needed to stop trying.

She probably should've been disappointed that he'd come here looking for Donovan and not her. She wasn't. It had gotten him here, hadn't it?

And maybe she should've been frustrated that Donovan had shown up right when she could've taken her seduction plan to the next level. She might've been if she hadn't expected it. Her brother had perfectly bad timing. Always. It was like he knew the exact moment to appear in order to protect Reilly's virtue from the one man Reilly'd had her heart set on for ... well, for a really freaking long time.

Not that she intended to let Donovan know of her major crush on Brady. Reilly was convinced Donovan still believed she was a virgin. Her parents certainly thought that so why wouldn't he? Hell, if Donovan only knew that she'd lost her virtue back in high school, there was a good chance he might need medication to moderate his blood pressure.

"Hey, Rye! You think you could hurry your ... um ... *butt* up? I'm headin' out."

There was only one reason her brother would censor his words. There was a customer in the store.

With her body back under control, Reilly hurried to the front of the store to see Donovan and Brady standing by the front door. Brady was halfway out of the building, but his eyes still lingered on her as she approached.

She grinned. "You realize you ring things up the same way you used to, right?"

Donovan rolled his eyes. "Whatever, twerp."

"Hey, hold up a minute," she told her brother as she went behind the register to ring up the guy who plopped down a box of Christmas lights.

"These are popular," she told the guy. She'd ordered them a week ago as one of those "just in case" items for the shelf, but she figured they would likely end up on the clearance shelf come January. She was shocked at how many people had come in to get one to avoid heading to the big box store.

"Eight sixty-five," she told him.

He handed her a ten-dollar bill. She got his change and passed it and the receipt to him.

"Merry, happy Chrismukkah," she told him.

His eyebrow quirked in question.

"It's a combo of Christmas and Hanukkah." She waved him off. "Happy holidays."

"Yeah, you, too," he said on his way out the door.

Once he was outside, she looked at Donovan. "You comin' back later or what?"

Donovan glanced at Brady before looking back at her. "I'm not sure. You need me to?"

She shrugged. "Probably not. That's like the third person who's been in here all day. I'll keep it open as long as we've got people comin' in, though. Or until those Christmas lights are gone."

It was Christmas Eve eve, or more accurately, two days before the big day, and it was the last night of Coyote Ridge's Holiday Festival. Once the vendors started setting up in the park, she didn't expect too many people to stop in. They'd gotten some residual traffic during the week since the tree was lit in Walker Park and residents were traipsing through the majestic light show every night, but it had died off last night. It was bound to happen because the food trucks that had become a hot commodity could handle most of the accommodations for those venturing into town to participate in the festivities.

On a positive note, Reilly could close down early and join the fun.

"Will we see you at the park tonight?" Donovan asked as he moved closer to the door.

"If you're lucky."

She ensured she caught Brady's gaze one last time before he disappeared for good.

The frown on his face amped up her smile even more.

One day, he was going to give in to his attraction to her. Brady pretended it didn't exist, but she knew better. Because of that, Reilly got great enjoyment out of riling him up whenever he was around.

When the store was empty once more, she connected her phone to the Bluetooth speaker behind the counter and got to work restocking the candy shelves. She was about to attempt to match Mariah Carey note for note when the bells over the door jingled. She tapped her phone to turn off the music and turned to greet the customer but found Tate standing with the door open wide, his eyes tracking something out of her view.

"What're you doin'?"

He held up a finger.

"Tate Bellamy Riggs. Are you stalkin' someone again?"

"Donovan and Brady are at Batter & Bliss. They're about to come out."

"Quit starin' at my brother," she told him, grinning wide.

"But he's so damn yummy." Tate walked in, letting the door close behind him. "Were they here?"

"For a minute."

"Man. I always miss the good stuff."

So he said. For some reason, Reilly had been under the impression Tate was avoiding her brother this past week. Ever since the birthday party, he'd been acting strange. Well, stranger than usual. When she tried to pry answers out of him, he told her it was nothing. She didn't believe him, but she was giving him the benefit of the doubt. She thought maybe he was still trying to deal with the fact his lying, cheating whore of an ex-boyfriend had come creeping around. As much as she wished Tate would never think about that guy again, she knew it wasn't that easy. Ben had really hurt Tate when he cheated.

"Where're they off to?" Tate asked as he approached.

Reilly shrugged. "Probably to brood and grumble."

That was what they were good at. Reilly wasn't sure what it was with all the guys in this town, but their grumpy meters seemed to be maxing out these days. Especially Brady's.

"They did say they'll be at the park tonight," she told Tate as she passed him a box of Hershey bars so he could make himself useful.

"Did you tell 'em you're gonna be there?"

"Where's the fun in that?" She tossed the empty box into the recycle bin behind the counter and grabbed another box. "Are you comin'?"

"Dunno."

"What do you mean you don't know?" she scolded. "I just told you Donovan's gonna be there. Now's your chance."

Tate's gaze darted away from her.

"Unless somethin' already happened," she told him, watching for any sign that he was keeping a secret from her.

When he didn't answer, she knew he was. Tate hated to lie to her, so he tended to bottle up whatever he didn't want her to know.

"Tate?"

"Hmm?"

"Did somethin' happen?"

His eyes slowly moved to her face. "It was nothin'."

Reilly stared, unable to hide her curiosity. "*What* was nothin'?"

Tate looked away, then quickly looked back, fidgeting with one of the chocolate bars. "Fine. I kissed Donovan."

She resisted the urge to squeal her delight. She was so happy for him, but based on his expression, he wasn't nearly as exuberant as she was.

"He won't even look at me now," Tate admitted, tossing the chocolate bar onto the shelf.

"Have you seen him since?"

"Only before we left the party. But he didn't look at me once after that."

"That doesn't mean anything."

Tate tilted his head to the side and raised his eyebrows. He definitely wasn't in agreement.

"It doesn't," she insisted. "You just—"

"It's fine, Rye," he said over her. "I'm over it. Plus, Ben called me last night."

Reilly went stone still as she lowered her hands and barely managed to hold onto the candy bars. "What?"

He nodded, but she knew he saw her hatred for his ex-boyfriend in her eyes.

"What did you tell him?"

"Nothing."

"Oh, Tate," she said, sighing dramatically. "Come on. Tell me you're not gonna fall for his shit."

"Can you blame a guy for not wanting to be alone on Christmas?"

No. She honestly couldn't. She was in the same boat. She didn't want to be alone on Christmas either. It seemed everyone in her family was happily paired up these days, and the last thing she wanted was to soak up all that lovey-dovey stuff without a little of her own to warm her at night.

However, she wasn't willing to spend the holiday with an ex who was a habitual cheater.

"It's been six months, Tate. Where's he been all this time?"

She knew the timeline because back when Tate had first learned that Ben was cheating on him, he'd gone to get tested for STDs. The initial test came back negative, but they told him to do a follow-up in ninety days because some diseases didn't show up that quickly. Which he did, and those tests came back negative, too. And God, she remembered him going through all that, terrified, and rightfully so. Reilly wanted to remind him of the hell Ben had put him through, but she also wanted to believe her best friend was smarter than that.

"Have you heard from him at all until the other day?"

"No." Tate passed her the empty box so she could toss it into the bin.

"So where's he been? Did he say?"

Tate didn't answer, and Reilly could tell she was irritating him. Good. She wanted to because the last thing she wanted was to watch Tate get his heart trampled on by a skeevy asshole like Ben.

"Probably screwin' half the guys in the next county, that's what he was doin'," she said when he didn't answer. "You know I'm right."

"He just wants to hang out," Tate admitted as he hopped up on the counter.

"I hope you told him to get fucked."

Tate laughed, but it sounded sad. "I guess it could be translated that way."

Reilly spun to face him and shook her head. "No."

Tate frowned. "No, what?"

"You are not gonna let Ben come over and stomp all over your trampled heart anymore."

"I'm not?"

"No."

"Why not?"

She grinned. "Because we agreed to stop sittin' on the sidelines this year."

"Reilly…"

"No excuses. Tonight's perfect. Donovan's gonna be at the park, and you can confront him then."

"And say what?"

She shrugged. "Tell him you wanna kiss him again. You want to, right?"

"Of course."

"Then stop pretendin' you don't and go after him."

"What about Brady? Did you happen to trap him under the mistletoe and not tell me about it?"

"Unfortunately, no." She met his gaze. "And you know me. I wouldn't've been able to keep it to myself."

She saw his remorse. She hadn't meant to make him feel bad.

"But I'm not givin' up, Tate." She smiled. "In fact, I know exactly what I need to do, and Brady McCord's not gonna know what hit him. So what do you say? One more shot?"

When Tate's eyebrow quirked, Reilly knew she had him.

Five

DONOVAN WANDERED THROUGH WALKER PARK, GREETING PEOPLE he knew. Friends, family, some he did business with. They were all out tonight.

Why wouldn't they be? It was a relatively warm, clear evening, and tomorrow was Christmas Eve. Coming here gave them a way to distract the kids so they weren't begging to open just one present early.

He smiled, remembering how he'd pulled that stunt on his parents every year. What started as a game instigated by him and his brothers had become a tradition by the time Chelsea was born. One present on Christmas Eve, but Mom and Dad got to pick. By the time Donovan was eight, they'd started allowing them to choose their own. Less tantrums that way when they didn't get exactly what they'd hoped for on the first try.

Donovan and Stone had both been in college by the time Reilly was capable of playing. And she took the prize for creativity. When she would open one, she would barter for another, and that girl knew how to haggle. And when she didn't get her way, she would turn to him and insist he make it happen. She'd latched onto him early, and Donovan had taken to her, too. Because of their significant age difference, he saw her differently than Stone, CJ, and Chelsea. They'd been pains in his ass. She'd been the sweet little doll everyone wanted to spoil rotten.

They still did, although she would never admit it.

Speaking of his sister. He figured Reilly was around there somewhere. He hadn't quite figured out what she was up to, but he got the feeling it had something to do with Brady. He knew when she set her sights on something, she didn't back down. And if Brady thought he could get the target off his back, he would have to work harder than he was. Donovan saw them in the store that morning. There was definitely something there.

Maybe this would be their year to figure it out.

His attention shifted to the enormous Christmas tree lit in the center of the park. He couldn't remember how tall it was, but he knew there'd been some sort of challenge for picking out the largest one. Not an easy feat in this neck of the woods where the soil wasn't favorable for pine trees to thrive. But somehow, they'd managed to find one that was awe-inspiring.

People were attempting to snap pictures of their loved ones in front of it, while some parents simply hoped their child wouldn't be the one to bring that thing crashing down. The high school choir was getting in their places up on the stage, preparing for their final Christmas production of the year, while food vendors were selling a variety of holiday goodies.

But Donovan wasn't there for the tree, the music, or the food. In fact, he wasn't sure why he was there at all. When he came up with the idea, he figured he and Brady would make an appearance, then swing by Moonshiners for a beer, but as usual, Brady backed out on him at the last minute. Donovan had expected as much and was doing his best to give Brady some breathing room. He couldn't imagine how difficult this year was for him with his mother gone.

Rather than go home and sulk alone, Donovan figured he could greet a few people he only saw this time of year, then slip out unnoticed if he was lucky.

"I didn't expect to see you out tonight," Curtis said as he approached. "Your mom and dad here?"

"Not tonight," Donovan told his uncle. "Mom was talkin' about gettin' dinner started early."

Aunt Lorrie chuckled. "I keep tellin' Owen to get you kids married off so they'll have someone to do it for them."

He knew Lorrie was only partly joking. At seventy-five, even after a severe health scare some years back, Lorrie was still front and center for every holiday meal with her brood. She was also responsible for keeping her kids coming around every Sunday for a family dinner. A tradition his family hadn't picked up, although they did make an effort to get together at least once every few months.

Donovan laughed. "She couldn't get that lucky. Plus, I think she likes goin' overboard with the pies. I tried to remind her Chelsea's vegan this year, and Stone cut out gluten, but she won't listen."

"What's gluten?" Curtis asked, his expression serious.

Lorrie waved Donovan off. "Don't answer that. I've told him a dozen times. Either he's not listenin', or he can't remember."

"I remember everything you've ever told me, darlin'," Curtis said, his tone low and gruff.

Donovan grinned.

"Brady come with you?" Curtis asked, glancing around and effectively changing the subject.

"No." Donovan sighed. "He's bein' a grinch this year. Probably sittin' at home in front of his drawing table."

"Well, that's too bad."

"Did you need him for somethin'?"

"Just thought I'd check in," Curtis said. "See how he's doin'."

Yep, everyone who knew Brady was thinking about him this year. This would be his second Christmas without her, and while Donovan hadn't been able to get Brady to agree to come to his folks' place last year, he wasn't going to let him back out this year.

"He's good," Donovan assured his uncle. "He's havin' dinner with us."

"That's good." Curtis nodded. "Real good."

"Hey, Donovan!"

"We won't keep you," Lorrie said, touching his hand. "Tell your mom I'll be stoppin' by next week to swap holiday dinner stories."

"I'll definitely tell her."

When they walked away, Donovan turned toward whoever had been calling him, but he wasn't sure who it was, so he started walking to see if someone got caught up in another conversation.

"I told you, that's not gonna happen."

The adamant tone of voice had Donovan looking around. It was then he saw Tate talking to someone. He couldn't see the guy's face, but there was something familiar about his cocky stance.

"No, I don't," Tate stated firmly, shrugging off the guy's hand.

Donovan kept walking, watching the pair. He drew up short when he reached the other side of them and could see who Tate was talking to.

What the fuck was Tate doing talking to that fucker? Donovan didn't know Tate's ex-boyfriend, but he knew what he looked like and enough about the guy not to like him. According to Reilly, the bastard had cheated on Tate too many times to count. And his philandering had caused Tate to go into a panic the last time. Donovan hadn't pushed Reilly for more information, but he'd learned enough to know that Tate had been concerned that the fucker had been screwing around without protection.

"Stop, Ben. I told you I'm willing to hang out, but that's it."

"What's goin' on?" Donovan asked as he approached, keeping his eyes on Ben as he stepped closer to Tate.

"Oh ... hey," Tate said with a sigh.

"Is there a problem?"

"No," Ben answered. "We were just leaving."

"No, we weren't," Tate told him and turned to walk away.

Tate didn't get two steps when Ben grabbed his arm.

Donovan intervened before he could think better of it. He grabbed Ben's wrist and gripped it firmly. Their eyes met and locked.

"I think he's good," Donovan told him. "You should go."

Ben released Tate's arm, so Donovan let him go. He grinned when Ben made a big production of adjusting the cuff on his pretentious coat. It was barely cold enough for a fucking coat and certainly not for those stupid fucking gloves.

"Is there something going on that I should know about?" Ben asked, gesturing between Donovan and Tate.

"Of course n—"

Donovan cut Tate off. "Our business ain't your business."

Ben's eyes widened, then narrowed to slits as he turned his attention to Tate. "Why do I even try?"

When Ben spun around and marched off, Tate huffed a laugh. "Why does *he* try? Good one."

"You okay?"

Tate's big blue eyes lifted to meet his, and that all too familiar mask fell into place. The one Tate used when he was putting on the charm and pretending nothing could hurt him.

"Of course I am, sweetie." Tate flashed a smile, but it looked forced. "As good as I'm gonna get, anyway. You didn't have to do that. I had it under control."

"I know," he lied, holding Tate's gaze.

Donovan knew his best option was to walk away. He never should've interfered in the first place. For the past few years, he'd been doing his best to steer clear of this exact scenario. He'd had a momentary lapse in judgment, which was the only way to explain what happened last weekend when he'd kissed the man. Donovan had made it a point to put it behind him.

Little good that had done.

He couldn't explain what it was about Tate that tripped his trigger, but Donovan had endured more than one fantasy about him. It never made sense because Tate wasn't the sort of man Donovan generally sought when he was looking to scratch the itch, but something definitely kept drawing him back in.

"Don't worry, sweetie," Tate said, smiling, and it looked a little less forced than before. "I'm a big boy. I can take care of myself."

And now Tate was back to his usual, playful self. It'd always made Donovan smile when Tate referred to someone as sweetie. And by someone, he meant everyone.

Before Donovan knew what he was doing, he stepped up to Tate, forcing him to tilt his head to stare up at him. "Can you?"

Tate's sharp inhale made Donovan's dick kick hard. "Can I what?"

"Take care of yourself?"

Tate's lips parted as though he wanted to say something, but words didn't come out.

Maybe *this* was what did it for him. Donovan's usual conquests were those who preferred to top but would give in when nudged the right way. But Tate ... no, Tate was a definite bottom, and if he had to guess, he would enjoy Donovan stripping him of all his control for one incredible night.

"I'm not scared of you," Tate said, his tone steady.

"I don't want you to be," he said, not backing off.

"No?"

"No." Donovan canted his head to the side. "I want you a lot of ways, but scared's not one of 'em."

He hadn't meant to say the words, but now that they were out there, Donovan couldn't see a reason to recall them. Tate was looking at him the same way he always did. With a bit of hero worship and a hell of a lot of lust sparkling in those big blue eyes. He was fucking adorable, and Donovan would thoroughly enjoy fucking him into submission.

Provided Tate understood he was only good for one night. That was all he had in him.

Tate didn't back down. "Does this alpha-hole thing work for you?"

Alpha-hole? That was new.

"Every time," he said honestly. "Does it work for you?"

Tate swallowed, his Adam's apple bobbing slowly in his throat. "Yeah," he rasped. "Yeah, it does."

"I thought so."

TATE WAS DREAMING.

That was the only way to explain this conversation he was having with Donovan freaking Jameson.

After what happened last weekend, Tate had expected Donovan to avoid him for the rest of his life. The guy couldn't even look at him after the kiss they'd shared in the hallway. To say it had hurt would've been an understatement.

Tate honestly had intended to move on with his life. He could check the Kiss Donovan Jameson box from his bucket list and call it good. He'd hoped he wouldn't have to tell Reilly about it because, while the kiss had been incredible, Tate hadn't wanted to think about it ever again. If he did, he would spend hours thinking about all the other things he wished he could do with Donovan, which would get him nowhere.

And yes, that was why he'd caved to Ben's follow-up invitation to come here tonight. He hadn't wanted to, but it was the only way he could keep from sulking at home and thinking about what he couldn't have.

He knew if he simply asked Reilly to stay home, she would have, but he wasn't that selfish. He wanted her to be happy, which was the only reason he'd agreed to be steadfast and straightforward in their approach and to make this the year they finally landed the men they wanted. Telling Reilly that it was too late for him would've put a damper on her mood, so he'd agreed even though he couldn't come up with a plan to make it happen.

Turned out he didn't need a plan. Evidently, he was on Santa's nice list this year because he was about to get everything he'd asked for—which just so happened to be six foot four inches of sin wrapped in layers of mouthwatering muscle and wearing a smirk that was most definitely naughty.

"What do you say, Tate? You think you're up for it?"

He almost asked Donovan what he was referring to but decided against it. He didn't care. He was up for anything this man was willing to dish out.

Tate nodded slowly, ensuring Donovan didn't misinterpret.

Another crooked grin formed on Donovan's sinful mouth. "Good. I need to stop by the store first."

Tate expected Donovan to lead the way, but he surprised him, placing his big hand on his lower back and urging him across the park toward the general store. It was closed for the night, but he figured Donovan didn't care. He had keys to the building. And if he didn't, Tate did since he often filled in for Reilly when she needed help.

Tate did his best to ignore the heat that seeped into his skin from Donovan's touch and the way his cock throbbed to the point of pain. He was so fucking hard he hurt.

When they entered the store, Donovan locked the door behind them and didn't flip on the lights. He guided Tate past the front register and down the aisle containing various personal items.

Tate was preoccupied with the hand that still lingered on his back. Otherwise, he would've gotten a clue before Donovan said, "Grab a box of condoms."

Do not freak out.

They're condoms.
They're your friend.
It's a good sign.
Grab a box.
Just pick one.
Just. Pick. One!

Hoping to shut that inner voice off, Tate turned to the shelf and reached for the first box he saw.

Donovan chuckled.

Tate looked up. That damn smirk was back.

"I don't think that size'll work."

"No?" *Jesus God. Why the hell did I ask that?*

"Would you like to measure?"

Oh, fuck.

Tate couldn't count how many fantasies he'd had about Donovan over the years. They'd started about the time he hit puberty, and the last one was … well, to be honest, it was last night. In the shower. He'd jacked off to thoughts of Donovan bending him over and… *Jesus God. This isn't happening!* Never … not one single time had he ever *ever* imagined Donovan suggesting he measure his penis.

Before he could formulate some sort of response, Donovan moved closer, his smirk turning into a full-fledged grin.

His gravel-laced voice scraped every nerve ending when he said, "You're fuckin' adorable. You know that?"

"No man's ever said that as a compliment before," Tate admitted, his voice far too hoarse. "Not to me, anyway."

Donovan touched his face, his big fingers curling around behind his head. "Now one has."

Their eyes met and held for so long Tate was expecting his alarm to go off at any second, and he would wake up to find the best dream he'd ever had was fading around the edges.

But his alarm didn't go off.

And it still didn't.

And then Donovan leaned in and kissed him.

For a moment, Tate was stunned. Too stunned to move. Too stunned to respond.

"If you don't kiss me back, I'm gonna have a complex," Donovan whispered against his lips.

Praying he wasn't going to make an ass of himself—more than he already had—Tate kissed him. Donovan didn't move this time, but he didn't let Tate go, either. He urged him closer as his lips parted, allowing Tate to take his time just like he had the last time. Tate noticed how Donovan's body and his grip hardened the deeper Tate's tongue went into his mouth until finally, Donovan groaned low in his throat and took over the kiss.

Tate saw stars behind his closed lids as Donovan kissed him with a passion he'd only ever imagined. Tate had kissed plenty of men in his twenty-four years, not to mention two girls back in high school. No one had ever kissed him like Donovan did. As though he was a meal meant to be savored, but he was too hungry to slow down long enough to do so.

The kiss worked to take his mind off where they were and who he was with. Tate let his hands join the party, sliding his fingers through the belt loops on Donovan's jeans and holding on for dear life.

He wanted this man to devour him whole. He wanted those giant hands to move over every inch of his body. He wanted Donovan to dominate him, to make him feel every ounce of the difference in their sizes. He wanted to feel the velvet smoothness of Donovan's giant cock against his tongue as he drove it deep into his throat. He wanted this man to boss him around like he was his freaking play toy. He wanted ... he wanted ... *he wanted*.

The kiss went nuclear when Donovan jerked him closer, gripping his ass with one big hand and grinding his hips against Tate's. The escalation had Donovan pushing him back, knocking him against the shelf, causing something to fall to the floor. Donovan pulled back first. He was breathing heavily, his eyes hooded. He looked as surprised as Tate felt, and he prayed it wasn't because he just realized who he was kissing.

"My sister's gonna kill me for this," Donovan muttered.

It was the equivalent of having ice water dumped over your head.

Tate stepped back. "Wow. If you can think about your sister at a time like this, clearly I'm not doin' somethin' right."

He'd meant it as a joke, but Donovan didn't take the bait, and Tate recognized the regret as soon as it flashed on Donovan's face.

Great.

"We should get back out there," Donovan said, taking the condoms and putting them back on the shelf.

And just like that, Tate's night went from bad to incredible and back to bad again.

Story of his life.

Six

AGAINST HIS BETTER JUDGMENT, BRADY HAD ALLOWED his ex-wife to convince him to go into town despite the fact he told Donovan he had too much work to catch up on and he wouldn't be going to Walker Park. He knew Donovan didn't believe him, but at least he didn't hassle him about it.

Brady couldn't say the same for Alyssa. According to her, he needed to get out of the house because he was becoming a bigger grump than usual. She blamed it on his inability to have fun, which, as it turned out, was part of the reason their marriage had failed.

The other part was because they'd simply fallen out of love with each other.

It happened, he figured. Two people met and got caught up in the whirlwind of life together. A year of enjoying every second in each other's company, then two more spent doing quick drive-bys in the kitchen on their way out the door. They'd finally stopped one day to reflect on what they'd become and realized, at some point, they had lost that spark.

Needless to say, the divorce was amicable, and they'd become pretty good friends over the past three years since everything fell apart. Alyssa had been there for him when his mother died last year, and though he'd tried to shut everyone out, both Alyssa and Donovan hadn't allowed him to. He knew that was what good friends did. They kept you together without you even realizing they were doing it.

It wasn't until Alyssa started dating Henry that Brady realized just how not in love with her he was. He probably should've felt an ounce of jealousy or perhaps a hint of remorse since she had once been his, but he felt nothing. He liked Henry, and the three of them had shared a few meals over the past year when Alyssa felt the need to check on Brady. He wasn't sure how Henry felt about Brady's friendship with her, but he seemed unfazed. Her happiness was all Henry appeared to care about, and Brady honestly wanted the best for Alyssa, so he hoped they worked out.

"You mind if we grab some hot chocolate?" Alyssa prompted when they neared the food trucks lined up on one side of the park.

"I'll get it for you, babe," Henry offered.

She smiled at him sweetly, her eyes glittering with love.

Brady shook his head and looked away, trying to find someone he could talk to so he could give Alyssa and Henry some time to themselves. He appreciated her need to keep him from sitting at home alone on a Saturday night. Still, for him, the only thing worse than sitting home alone and watching the Christmas movie marathons that were running on every channel was being a third wheel to his ex-wife.

Luckily, he caught sight of Donovan across the way, and he sighed his relief. "I'm gonna talk to D. I'll catch up with y'all later."

Alyssa's little crooked smirk told him she knew exactly what he was doing.

"Have fun," she said. "Say hello to Reilly for me."

"What?"

She giggled loudly, then hurried off after Henry.

Shaking his head, he started in the direction he saw Donovan.

"I'm startin' to think you're followin' me."

Brady followed the sound of her voice and found Reilly moving swiftly toward the gingerbread funhouse, their paths crossing with only a few feet between them.

"You'd know it if I was," he told her, doing his best not to look at her legs. She was wearing a skirt and a pair of those fluffy-lined boots that seemed to be all the craze these days. Her boots went to about mid-calf and her skirt about mid-thigh, leaving quite a bit of her lovely, toned legs uncovered.

"Eyes up here, cowboy," she said, and he realized she was walking backward, continuing away from him as he stared.

When he met her gaze, she winked, then crooked her finger, inviting him to join her.

Brady shook his head, but he didn't outright reject her. Following her was a bad idea. All day, he'd been battling thoughts of her. More specifically, of that morning at the general store when he'd touched her. It hadn't been at all like the times in the past when he was able to think of Reilly as Donovan's little sister. Brady wasn't sure whether it was the moment or simply some sort of hiccup in the space-time continuum, but what he'd felt wasn't remotely close to sisterly affection for the woman who had taunted him for years.

"Are you scared, cowboy?"

Yes. Yes, he was.

But not of her. He knew she was screwing with him because that was what Reilly did. She'd been doing it for years. What scared him was this insane desire he felt when he looked at her. It had been a long damn time since he'd felt something quite this … powerful. He feared it was more powerful than his ability to resist her, and he had a hell of a motivation to do that. As he continued to remind himself her brother was his best friend. He could only imagine the fallout that would happen if he were to entertain the notion of dating Donovan's little sister.

Speaking of Donovan.

Brady looked across the park in the direction he'd seen him a few minutes ago. He was no longer there, so he searched the familiar faces around him until—

Was that Donovan and Tate going toe to toe in the middle of the park?

"Your loss, cowboy," Reilly called out.

Brady jerked his attention from the two men squaring off and turned it to Reilly as she spun around and kept walking. When she reached the gingerbread house, she put her hand on the doorframe and glanced back at him, gifting him with one of her seductive smiles.

"You can't do this," he muttered under his breath even as he started following her. "It's stupid. *You're* stupid."

Goddamn. What the fuck was he thinking?

Knowing he was going to regret this but unable to stop his legs from moving, Brady followed her into the gingerbread house.

It was an actual two-story frame of a house built out of pre-made wooden forms designed to connect without screws or nails. The decor that made it look like a real gingerbread house was added after the fact. Since it was outside, the town opted not to use food-grade products in the design but rather to make it appear as though it was, so it only looked like candy. That didn't stop some people from attempting to eat it.

Brady stopped at the door and peered inside. There were three different rooms, all on the lower floor since the second story was merely for show on the exterior. One room had a Christmas tree and a rocking chair set up beside a faux fireplace. Another was designed to be a kitchen, with appliances made of wood for the kids to play with if they wanted. It was also where they stashed the cookies—real ones that were replenished as they disappeared—for Santa. The last room had a sofa made of wood and foam and wrapped in white felt, making it look more like a giant marshmallow train.

Brady was familiar with the house because he was the one who had designed it. The exterior, anyway. Being that he was an architect, the mayor came to him with a design idea and asked if he would help in creating something that they could reuse year after year. He'd taken her idea and worked with some family friends—Wolfe and Lynx Caine—who built furniture for a living for the actual creation of it. This was the town's second year using the house, and it had held up relatively well so far.

Brady stepped into the house and glanced into each room, which were all visible from every angle. Meaning there was absolutely no privacy. He found Reilly standing near the Christmas tree, her smile amped up to twenty as she stared back at him.

"I won't bite," she said as he neared. "Unless you want me to."

Sighing, Brady moved closer as he heard more people coming in behind him. "You're wastin' your breath, girl."

"You realize I'm not a girl anymore, right?" she countered, cocking her hip.

He kept his eyes trained on her face. "Trust me. I'm well aware."

When he stopped three feet away, she crooked her finger again.

Curious what her intention was, he moved closer. There were kids in the kitchen, likely pillaging the cookies, but for the moment, they had the room to themselves.

"As long as we're on the same page," she said, her voice huskier than before.

He held her stare, trying to come up with the right words to say to convince her to back off. She was taunting a very desperate man, and she had no idea what she was doing. He had no business with a woman like Reilly. She was too sweet, too innocent for the likes of him.

Reilly lifted her hand and pointed toward the ceiling. It took a moment for Brady to realize what she was doing. When he tipped his head back, he saw the mistletoe dangling overhead.

"You don't want to buck tradition, do you?" she whispered when he brought his head to level once again.

Damn that mistletoe.

REILLY WAS SURPRISED THE RUSE HAD WORKED.

Of course, Brady hadn't given in yet, but based on the heat blazing in his eyes, she figured it was only a matter of time.

To help him out, she took one step closer. Her boot bumped the toe of his shoe.

"You know I can't kiss you, right?" His voice rumbled like thunder through her insides.

"Because you're a bad kisser, and you'll lick my makeup off?" she teased, grinning as she cocked her head.

His left eyebrow cocked, daring her to keep it up.

"Your lips are broken?" She giggled.

"No."

"Ah. Are you scared?" He wasn't, she knew. But it was worth a shot since it seemed to have worked to get him in here.

Brady reached up and touched her hair, his gaze following the movement. For a second, she thought he was going to cup her face and kiss her, but he merely twirled one lock around his finger before meeting her gaze again.

He tugged gently on her hair, and she felt the sensual pull between her legs.

"Donovan'll kill me, Reilly." His voice was so low she barely heard it over the chatter coming from the other room.

She leaned in. "He doesn't have to know."

It wasn't what she wanted to say, but it was the only thing she could think of.

"He'll know."

Reilly made a point of peering around him, pretending to search for her brother. She knew he wasn't there, but she was trying to make a point. When she met his brooding dark stare again, she raised her eyebrows. "He's not here."

Brady closed the distance between them. "He'll know because kissing you once won't be enough."

She shivered from the arousal that coursed through her at his gruffly spoken promise.

Oh, God. She wanted him to kiss her. But as soon as she tilted her head, angling her lips toward his, he shifted, his mouth moving closer to her ear.

"I won't be satisfied until I've kissed you everywhere," he breathed against her cheek. "And I do mean everywhere, Reilly."

Reilly grabbed his sleeve in an attempt to keep herself upright. Her knees were weak, and adrenaline was flooding her system. She'd wanted to hear him say things like that for so long. For years, she'd been infatuated with this man. She'd never allowed it to get in the way of their friendship or other relationships she'd tried on for size, but every time she broke up with someone, her focus came right back to him.

And here they were. Both single. Both obviously interested. Why was he fighting this?

Reilly decided not to press him for more. As much as she wanted him, she wasn't that girl. And she never would be. Call her old-fashioned, but she wanted him to make the first move, and she'd already done her part in showing him she would be receptive.

"Fine," she whispered against his cheek. "If you don't want me, I'm sure there's someone else who—"

The last words died on her tongue because Brady crushed his mouth to hers. His hand curled behind her head, the other across her lower back, holding her in place as he took a deep breath and then licked along the seam of her lips. Reilly didn't resist. She couldn't. Brady McCord was kissing her, and it was so much better than she'd ever dreamed. And boy had she dreamed about it.

She whimpered, leaning into him and sliding her tongue against his. She was still fisting the sleeve of his shirt to keep her balance, but she wasn't going anywhere. He had one hand still palming her head, the other banded around her waist, and just like that morning, there was no mistaking his arousal. It was hot and heavy between them.

"You don't tempt a starving man with filet mignon and then threaten to take it away, darlin'."

She was filet mignon? Wow. She would've settled for being a New York strip, but that…

Someone cleared their throat. Reilly remembered they were standing inside the gingerbread house in the middle of Walker Park. Families were out to enjoy the festivities, which meant there were likely kids watching.

Before she could step away from Brady, he took her hand and turned her so that she was in front of him. He guided her past the parents who pretended not to notice them making out while their two-year-old admired the Christmas tree.

Brady's fingers twined with hers, and he curled them inward, holding her hand as he steered her out of the gingerbread house and around to the side.

"You're dangerous," he said, his eyes smoldering as they peered into hers.

"I could say the same about you."

As they stood there, her hand still in his, Reilly knew he was going to come up with an excuse as to why that could never happen again. And it wouldn't be too hard considering she was related to his favorite excuse—his best friend Donovan.

But before he could, she scrounged for as much courage as she could muster and decided to throw him a curveball.

"If you never want to kiss me again, that's fine," she said, keeping her voice level. "But if you use my brother as your reasoning, I can promise you, Brady McCord, it *will* never happen again."

"No?"

"In case you haven't noticed, I'm a grown-ass woman. I don't live at home. I don't rely on my brothers, my sister, or my parents to pay my bills. I've got a job—no, I *own* my own business because my daddy entrusted me to operate the general store because no one else wanted it. So don't think it's up to Donovan who I do or do not kiss."

With that off her chest, she stood there and waited for him to make a decision. She only hoped he couldn't hear the heavy thud of her heart. There was no doubt it was going to crack right down the middle if he rejected her now, and since he was holding her hand, she couldn't very well cross her fingers and hope to God he wouldn't be an idiot.

So she waited and hoped she was on Santa's nice list this year. And while she was hoping, she decided she hoped Brady McCord was on the naughty list because, damn, wouldn't that be fun?

REILLY WAS RIGHT.

Deep down, Brady knew she was a grown-ass woman, as she so eloquently put it. She could make her own decisions, but she didn't understand that it wasn't about seeking permission from her brother. That wasn't the point. It was about not betraying that kind of trust with his best friend. Donovan expected Brady to respect his family, and to do that, Brady had to walk away from this.

There was no denying he wanted her. More than oxygen at the moment. But what sort of man would he be if he simply took what he wanted without regard to the consequences or boundaries? His mother had raised him better than that.

"I'm sorry, Reilly," he said softly.

Based on her expression, that was the last thing she expected him to say. Her eyes widened, and her lips parted. Twice, she opened her mouth, probably to blast him, only to close it again.

It took about ten seconds as the information registered in her brain, but then the sassy woman he deeply cared about returned, and her eyes sparkled with mischief.

"Your loss, Mr. McCord," she said with a sauciness he found so fucking hot.

Yes, it most definitely was.

"Maybe, if you're lucky, I'll see you around," she said before pivoting on her heel and walking away. He watched, admiring the sexy sway of her delectable ass and hating himself for being a stand-up guy.

Then again, a woman as incredible as Reilly Jameson wouldn't want him if he weren't. She wouldn't have looked at him twice.

At least there's that.

Seven

DONOVAN WAS AN ASSHOLE; THAT WAS ALL there was to it. He could admit it.

He'd kissed Tate, then panicked and walked away.

Not immediately, of course. He'd been unable to simply run out of the store without ensuring Tate was okay. Of course, his concern had earned him a glare from the much younger man before Tate stormed off toward the parking lot. As soon as Donovan saw Tate's Mustang pull out of the lot, he headed for his truck.

Thankfully, he didn't listen to his dick and follow Tate home. That would've made him a complete asshole. Instead, he'd come home to lick his wounds and ridicule himself for his stupidity.

"You're an idiot," Donovan muttered as he paced his kitchen. "What the fuck is wrong with you?"

The last time he second-guessed himself was nearly twenty years ago, back when he'd been young and stupid and thought he knew every damn thing about every damn thing. He'd been in love with a man who had loved him deeply and honestly, but Donovan's hubris had gotten in the way. Rather than embrace that love, he'd wondered whether or not he was ready to be tied down.

For nearly twenty years, Donovan regretted not taking the leap because he'd spent the past two decades hopping from one random bed to another, knowing that it would only be for a brief moment. Yeah, he'd dated a few men along the way, but nothing that had ever resembled anything close to love. He'd ruined it. He'd given up his chance because he'd worried he was making the wrong decision. If he hadn't been so stupid, he could've still been sharing the same bed with a man he loved. But his uncertainty had led them down different paths. That man—whose name he couldn't even think of without feeling more guilt—was happily married with three kids, and Donovan … well, he was still looking.

There was no way Tate Riggs was his second chance. He couldn't be. Just because Donovan had that strange, giddy sensation when he was near Tate didn't mean anything. It was probably an early-onset mid-life crisis or something. The guy was fifteen years younger, for fuck's sake. Not to mention, not at all Donovan's type. He was cute and sweet and…

"You're supposed to be talking yourself *out* of this asinine idea," he said, thrusting his hand through his hair.

He groaned and tilted his head back, unable to fight off the memory of that damn kiss. That kiss was supposed to be a precursor to another brief fling, but something happened, something that triggered his morality, and he'd been forced to walk away from Tate because spending even a single night in bed with Tate and then having to face the man for years to come wasn't something he could live with.

He figured if you asked Tate, he would tell you Donovan ran away with his tail between his legs. That hadn't been the case, but he figured it sure as shit might look like it.

"Damn it."

Now that he was home, he should've been able to put it all behind him. So he'd kissed Tate. So fucking what? It wasn't like he'd signed a contract promising more than that. It was a spur-of-the-moment thing—so what if it happened twice?—and now he was over it.

"Over it," he grumbled.

He was so not over it but damn it to hell. If he tried to talk to Tate now, the guy would slam the door in his face. And the worst part was Donovan deserved it. What the fuck was he thinking? Kissing that kid. Jesus.

And fine, Tate was so not a kid anymore. At least from a chronological perspective. Donovan knew that. But compared to thirty-nine, twenty-four was still a kid. What the hell could they possibly have in common aside from some intense physical attraction? And attraction damn sure wasn't a problem. Donovan wasn't sure his dick had ever been as hard as it was when he thought about all the dirty things he wanted to do to Tate.

He went to the living room and flopped on the couch. The lights were off, but he didn't care. He sat because he was tired of wearing a hole in the damn floor. He stared at the darkened Christmas tree. He'd half-assed it this year but gave himself props for making the effort. He'd pulled the tree out of storage, set it up, and plugged it in. If it weren't pre-lit, he would've simply had a tree in his living room because he didn't do anything more. There were no ornaments or tinsel or strings of popcorn like on his parents' tree. Then again, he had no one to share the holiday with. Other than family, Donovan was alone.

He was so fucking tired of being alone.

His thoughts instantly wandered back to that damn kiss.

Fuck.

He'd been right about Tate giving up control. He'd done it so easily, and for some damn reason, that had turned Donovan on more than anything else ever had. There'd been no duplicity in that kiss. Tate hadn't been angling for something from him. It had been genuine, and … goddamn, it had been sweet.

Donovan wasn't sure which he hated himself more for: kissing Tate or walking away from him. Both made for a shitty existence.

What made it impossibly worse was the fact that Tate had looked at him as though he'd lost his damn mind. And maybe he had. At the time, he appreciated Tate's ability to walk away without confrontation. Now that he was home, Donovan realized what that meant. Tate didn't care one way or the other, and yeah, that fucking hurt more than he wanted to admit.

He sat up and put his elbows on his knees, dropping his head into his hands.

He had two options.

One, he could go to bed and pretend today never happened.

Or two, he could go to Tate's and apologize for being an asshole. That was the least Tate deserved.

Or—because why shouldn't there be a third fucking option?— he could go to Tate's, apologize, and convince him to give Donovan one more chance.

And then what? How the hell would he be able to tell Tate that he wasn't looking for one night, but he couldn't promise anything more? It would sound like bullshit.

"Because it is," he whispered.

He was tired of too-brief affairs that left him wanting more.

Donovan took a deep breath and got to his feet. He marched toward the kitchen, grabbed his keys, phone, and wallet from where he'd left them on the counter. He grabbed his coat on the way to the garage, refusing to second-guess himself again.

This had to be done.

Twenty minutes later, he drove past his parents' house toward the barn behind it. He considered pulling around to the back so his mom and dad didn't see his truck parked there but decided he didn't give a shit. He hadn't been in the closet for decades. Not since he accepted for himself that he was gay. As soon as he did, he came out to his parents, knowing full well they would support him. They had, and he hadn't looked back. Not once. He wasn't about to start hiding again now.

He parked behind Tate's Mustang, which was at the side of the barn in the same spot he always parked. Reilly's truck was gone, so he hoped that meant Tate was home, but he could've easily left with her in the past forty-five minutes, meaning this would be a wasted trip.

Rather than race to the door, Donovan stared at the decorations in the yard and grinned. They reminded him so much of his sister. Reilly was a little ball of chaos. He never knew what was going to come out of her mouth because her brain wasn't wired like everyone else. She knew what she wanted and didn't make excuses for it. She did what pleased her, not everyone else. When asked to join the swim team in high school, she turned them down because she wasn't interested in team sports. When Mom and Dad had wanted her to go to college, she'd bucked the system, claiming she would rather spend her time learning life lessons than going to keggers with her roommate while fighting for good grades.

He'd always loved her spirit. And he loved how uninhibited she was. Even if it meant she paired a fifteen-foot-tall inflatable snowman with a three-foot-tall wire reindeer. They didn't go together at all, yet they seemed to be a good match.

Kinda like him and Tate.

Donovan briefly wondered how much Tate had contributed to the decor. Very little, if he had to guess. Like everyone else, Tate let Reilly be Reilly and simply enjoyed being in her life. He was a good guy, that was for sure. A damn good friend to her.

But besides knowing his character, Donovan had paid too little attention to Tate. And he had a good reason. For a while now, Donovan had been fighting this attraction. He knew it wouldn't work, and the last thing he wanted was to hurt the guy or piss off his sister when he did. Yes, Donovan was selfish, but he'd never been one to forsake the important things. Like his friendship with Reilly or, by proxy, his friendship with Tate.

"No second-guessing," he told himself, shutting off the truck and getting out.

He walked up the path to the front door, noticing the little Christmas tree with twinkling lights sitting on the porch. He stared at the double red doors they'd designed to look like barn doors and forced himself to knock.

A minute passed.

He knocked again.

Another minute passed, and he figured Tate was standing on the other side of that door waiting for him to leave, or he wasn't home. Either way, Donovan looked like an idiot.

He turned to go. As soon as he did, he heard the deadbolt unlock.

When he turned back, he found Tate standing there, staring back at him with confusion etched on his handsome face. His shaggy blond hair was mussed, and he was wearing red and green plaid pajama pants and a T-shirt that read: PLEASE STOP ASKING FOR THE PERFECT MAN FOR CHRISTMAS... THREE TIMES THIS WEEK, SANTA TRIED TO KIDNAP ME.

That shouldn't be sexy, but Jesus. It kinda was.

"She's not here," Tate said.

"I wasn't lookin' for her."

If he was surprised by that admission, Tate didn't show it.

"I came by to apologize," Donovan said as he moved closer. "For what happened earlier."

"For kissing me?" Tate retorted. "Or for bein' a pussy and runnin' away?"

Donovan deserved that.

He took another step toward Tate until he was standing at the threshold. Tate didn't back down; he merely tilted his head and maintained eye contact.

"I'm not big on regrets, Donovan, so if you need to apologize to make yourself feel better, you're good. I don't care. You can—"

"Shut up, Tate," he whispered, reaching for him.

Donovan cupped his face with both hands, tilted his head, and kissed him. Tate didn't hesitate the way he had earlier. He gripped the front of Donovan's shirt and held on, their tongues thrashing. Donovan managed to step into the house and close the door behind him before Tate dragged him along, moving deeper into the house.

"Tate, you should know—"

"Don't make promises you don't intend to keep," Tate said, pulling Donovan into his bedroom and closing the door.

Donovan didn't have time to look around before Tate shoved him onto the bed, moving over him.

"I don't need your promises, and I don't want them," Tate said, straddling his hips and kissing him.

The guy was giving Donovan the out he usually sought, but for the first time in twenty years, he didn't need it. He didn't feel the urge to limit this to a single moment in time. No, he made no promises about tomorrow, but he wasn't putting an expiration date on this either.

Tate shoved at Donovan's jacket, attempting to get it off. It was then Donovan realized their positions were reversed. It was enough to have him groaning as he sat up, grabbing Tate around the waist and holding him in place so he didn't fall to the floor.

"Take your shirt off," Donovan growled, taking back the reins.

Tate pulled back enough to meet his gaze as he reached behind his head and grabbed a fistful of cotton before dragging it off.

That was more like it. Tate wasn't bulky, but the man was ripped. He knew he didn't get that body being an EMT, but he certainly took care of himself in his downtime.

Donovan pressed his hand flat on Tate's back, his fingers spanning from one shoulder blade to the other. Why did that turn him on so much? He'd never been into smaller men, but Tate … yeah, Tate did it for him. Donovan leaned in, kissing along Tate's collarbone, nipping his pectoral muscle, then sliding lower to tease Tate's nipple.

"Oh, fuck," Tate hissed, his arms wreathing Donovan's head and holding him in place.

Donovan bit his nipple, reveling in Tate's hiss.

In one swift move, Donovan stood up, holding onto Tate before spinning around and dropping him onto the bed, moving over him. He planted his knee between Tate's legs and leaned forward, bringing his mouth to Tate's. He kissed him. Only once. Gently. Then he stood tall and took a moment to admire the man he was going to do naughty, *naughty* things to.

TATE'S BLOOD WAS RUSHING IN HIS EARS.

He was light-headed but doing his best not to react. He wasn't sure what had compelled Donovan to come here, but as soon as he'd seen the man standing on the porch, Tate had vowed he would not have a repeat of what happened earlier at the store. If this was an early gift from Santa, by God, Tate was going to unwrap it and play with it before Santa realized he'd left it at the wrong house.

No, he didn't want any promises, but regardless of what tomorrow brought, tonight wasn't going to end with Donovan walking away. Not if he had anything to say about it.

Tate watched as Donovan stripped off his jacket and placed it on the desk chair that sat in the corner. His green eyes glittered in the overhead light as his gaze raked over Tate. He could practically feel the man touching every inch of him, and he wasn't close enough to do so.

His heart pounded harder when Donovan toed off his boots, then freed the buttons on his cuffs before he began to unbutton his shirt slowly. He caught glimpses of Donovan's heavily muscled chest, the dark spattering of hair as his hands moved lower. When Donovan had the shirt open, Tate held his breath, eager for him to take it off, but he didn't.

Maybe that wasn't so bad for now. Tate wouldn't deny that he was known to drool over Donovan. The man's rock-hard body had been turning his head since he was a teenager. Everything about the man turned him on. He was just so damn big, so masculine. So rugged. Tate had fantasized more than once about being manhandled by this beautiful, sexy man.

Donovan moved slowly. Like a jungle cat getting ready to pounce. Only he didn't. He simply leaned forward, maintaining eye contact as he hooked his fingers in the waistband of Tate's pajama pants and slowly slid them down his legs. When Tate's cock sprang free, Donovan's gaze shifted lower. He instantly wondered whether he measured up to any of the men Donovan had dated in the past, and Tate knew there had been many. None of those he knew about had been like Tate. Completely and totally average. Not only his cock, but the rest of him as well. Donovan tended to go for the muscle-bound linebacker types who could likely hold their own with him. Tate was not in the same league. Not by a long shot.

Feeling a tad self-conscious, Tate reached down to cover his cock.

Before he could, Donovan gripped his wrist. "That belongs to me now."

Tate inhaled sharply.

"Unless you've got a problem with that."

It wasn't a question, but he could tell Donovan was gauging Tate's reactions, probably to see how far he could take it.

"No. Definitely no problem," he said, wanting to assure him he had no concerns about belonging to this man. Even for only a little while.

"Good," Donovan said as he curled his enormous fist around Tate's cock. His fingers overlapped, but based on the gleam in Donovan's eyes, he approved.

Finally, Donovan's gaze slowly moved back to his face, and a smirk formed. "No matter what I do, you don't come without asking me nicely. Understand?"

Tate nodded, even as he wondered whether he was capable of holding back. He'd never been this turned on before.

The next thing Tate knew, Donovan was on his knees at the side of the bed, his arms curled around Tate's thighs as he easily pulled him to the edge of the bed. It seemed effortless on Donovan's part, and holy shit, that was so freaking hot. But not nearly as much as it was when Donovan began kissing and licking his cock and balls, tormenting him with his warm breath.

It was all Tate could do to breathe. The pleasure was intense. The attention was overwhelming. There was no doubt Donovan was experienced, and he knew exactly how to lick and suck to make Tate moan. He never rushed; there was no edging involved. Donovan didn't push him to the brink and bring him back down. He simply savored, alternating between sucking his cock and his sac, then kissing along the inside of his thigh, the stubble on his jaw abrading Tate's skin in the most delicious way.

When Tate whimpered, Donovan stopped, joining him on the bed, moving over him. Tate reached for him, eager to be an equal participant. He slid his hands inside Donovan's shirt, his palms gliding over warm skin, the soft hair on his chest slipping between Tate's fingers, those delicious muscles shifting beneath his touch. Donovan kissed him again. Slower this time.

"It's gonna be a long night," Donovan whispered against his mouth. "I will have licked every inch of you and made you come with my hands, my mouth, and my cock before you ever see the light of day."

"Yes, please," Tate whimpered, curling his leg around Donovan's thigh, trying to pull him closer.

Donovan grinned against his lips. "No need to rush. Just enjoy."

Oh, he fully intended to. Hell, the night could end now, and this would qualify as the most intense night of Tate's life. He didn't even want to think about what that said about his previous encounters.

Donovan sat up and pulled his shirt off his arms, letting it slide down until it fluttered to the floor behind him.

Tate reached for the button on his jeans, moving slowly, waiting to see if Donovan would stop him. When he didn't, he flipped it free, then lowered the zipper. The head of Donovan's cock was right there, the tip glistening over the waistband of his boxer briefs. Tate licked his lips, his mouth watering to taste him.

Donovan must've read his mind because his eyes flashed hot, and a moment later, he was off the bed, stripping his jeans down his legs. Tate lifted up, watching, waiting with eager anticipation. When Donovan stood tall, gloriously naked, Tate inhaled sharply. The man was sinfully beautiful. His cock was a far cry from average. Nine inches? Ten? And thicker than any that Tate had ever encountered.

"You'll take me. Don't worry," Donovan said as he joined him on the bed again. "And it'll be good for both of us."

Tate had a feeling he was sincere in that. And for the first time in a long time, he trusted the man he was with. Not with his heart. Never that. But definitely with his body.

"Come here," Donovan said, curling his hand behind Tate's head as he rolled to his back, pulling Tate with him.

Tate straddled his hips, their cocks rubbing together, making Tate see stars once again. He planted his hands beside Donovan's head and groaned when Donovan gripped his ass with both hands, rocking him forward and back, increasing the friction between their erections.

"Kiss me, Tate."

Heat bloomed in his entire body as he kissed Donovan, whimpering and moaning as the sensations intensified. It was more intimate than sex, this slow grind, the way Donovan's fingers spread his ass cheeks apart, teasing him lightly.

When he pulled back to catch his breath, he met Donovan's stare and grinned.

"Why're you smilin'?"

"Because this … it feels so good."

"Just wait, little boy."

Oh, man. Should that be such a turn-on? It was. It so definitely was.

"It gets better," Donovan tacked on.

Tate wasn't sure that was even possible, but he was damn sure eager to find out.

Eight

An hour and a half after Reilly left him at the gingerbread house, Brady pulled down the Jamesons' driveway, continuing past the main house toward the barn.

It felt weird not to stop because, except when they'd been helping to design the barndominium, Brady had never parked back here. He always spent his time at the main house, where he'd practically grown up. That house wasn't overflowing with kids these days, but the family still got together often, and Brady was usually right there in the thick of things.

That was what bothered him. Not that he'd been a part of the family for so long, but that Reilly probably didn't understand his reason for putting the brakes on. He needed her to understand. Which was why he was here. He wanted to explain, to ensure she didn't hate him. He wanted her. There was no denying that. But it felt like crossing a line, and he didn't want to be that guy. He didn't want to take advantage of the sweetest woman he'd ever known. He hoped if he explained it that way, they could move past this and still be friends.

As he pulled up to the barn, he frowned. Donovan was here? Why? Had Reilly called him? Was she that pissed at Brady that she would call her brother to … to what? Give him grief over Brady's decision?

Shit.

He parked behind Donovan's truck and considered turning around and going home. The last thing he wanted was to get into an argument over right and wrong with those two. He'd witnessed a few of their knock-down drag-outs over the years, and simply put, he would prefer to be anywhere else when those two got into a shouting match.

"Fuck me," he grumbled as he turned off the SUV.

If those two were arguing because of him, it was his responsibility to set them straight.

He opened his door and got out, closing the door as he glanced at the land that backed up to a quiet neighborhood. It wasn't always quiet. In fact, it had become one of the more popular areas in town, the section of town where the younger Millennials of Coyote Ridge were congregating as they plotted to take over the world. At least, that was the running joke because some of those youngsters were stepping up to the plate where the town was concerned.

Brady grinned. At what point had he considered anyone a youngster? When had he gotten that fucking old? He wasn't quite forty. Not for another year. It wasn't like he was over the hill or some shit.

Taking a deep breath, he headed up the porch to the house, bypassing the enormous inflatable snowman and the tiny wire reindeer beside it. The large porch had been decked out for the holidays, draped in garland and lights. There was even a small Christmas tree with colorful twinkling lights. On either side of it were rocking chairs where he imagined Reilly and Tate sat when they were drinking coffee or maybe at night with a glass of wine. He could picture them there. Those two certainly were a pair.

That gave him pause. Damn near all her life, Reilly and Tate had been ... well, for lack of a better word, they'd been together. Not romantically, he knew, but inseparable all the same. What would happen if he did want a relationship with her? Would he have to fight Tate for her time? Brady was too old to do that.

He wasn't looking for some long, drawn-out relationship. He wanted a woman he could spend the rest of his life with, and since he wasn't getting any younger, the next woman he brought to his bed, he intended to keep there for eternity. That was the reason he'd avoided dating for the past couple of years. Yeah, he'd dated a few women during that time, but no one who'd held his interest long enough to make it past a first date. He wasn't opposed to it. Not in the least, but he didn't look forward to it either. Getting to know someone over dinner and drinks, finding out whether they had anything in common or were even compatible, sounded worse than spending his nights alone.

With Reilly, he wouldn't have to worry about that. He knew everything there was to know about her. And vice versa. Mostly. But Reilly was only twenty-three. She was too young to settle down, right? Brady didn't even know how she felt about marriage or kids. Did she want either? Both? When?

Before knocking, he glanced at his watch to ensure it wasn't too late to be dropping by. It wasn't quite ten, so he figured it was still socially acceptable. As for whether Reilly would want to see him or not … that was something else entirely.

Brady knocked on the door and took several steps back, waiting patiently.

When the door opened, Reilly appeared. Her dark hair was in a messy pile on top of her head, her face scrubbed clean, and a pair of headphones curled around her neck as though she'd taken them off to deal with him. She was no longer wearing the dick-hardening skirt and boots. What she *was* wearing wasn't much better. A pair of cotton shorts, an oversized sweatshirt that hung off one shoulder, and slippers that looked very much like the boots she had on earlier.

Christ Almighty. The woman was going to give him a heart attack.

"What?" she asked, holding the door as she stared back at him.

"Can we talk?"

Her eyebrows lifted slowly. "I'm pretty sure you said everything you needed to say earlier."

"Come on, Reilly."

She glanced back into the house. "It's not a good time."

"I know Donovan's here. If you two are arguing—"

Reilly huffed a laugh. "You think my brother's here for me?" She tapped the headphones. "Oh, no. He's here enjoying himself with my *best friend.*"

Brady frowned as he tried to process what she was saying. Donovan and Tate? Since when?

"You don't see me gettin' all butthurt over that, do you?" she snapped. "But hey. I'm evolved. I believe people should be allowed to make their own decisions." She gripped the door and stepped back. "I'll see you around, Brady."

Before she could shut the door in his face, he put his hand on the wood. Her eyes widened as she stared up at him.

He couldn't walk away from her. He should have. That was a given. But he couldn't.

From somewhere in the house, Brady heard a loud grunt followed by laughter. Donovan's laughter.

Jesus.

Reilly rolled her eyes and reached for her headphones. "If you don't mind, I need to drown out the sound or—"

"Come home with me," he blurted before he could think better of it.

"What?"

"You heard me, Reilly. Don't make it weird."

"An hour ago, you were being all noble and shit. Now you want to be my knight in shining armor because my best friend and my brother are…" She waved her hand behind her. "If it's all the same to you, I'd rather suffer here."

Brady took a step toward her. He had one foot in the house, one on the porch, and he was face to face with the woman he couldn't stop thinking about.

"Trust me when I tell you, the things I want to do to you do not make me anyone's knight."

Her lips parted with a soft gasp.

"Come home with me," he whispered.

"What happened to bein' all noble and shit?" she snapped.

Fuck noble. Brady cupped her face and kissed her. He knew it was wrong, but he couldn't help it. He couldn't remember wanting a woman the way he wanted her.

"Come home with me," he repeated, enunciating the words slowly.

"Why? So you can send me home in the mornin'?" She shook her head. "I have no desire to do the walk of shame from Brady McCord's house."

He moved closer until her breasts were pressing against his chest, and her head was tipped back so she could still look into his eyes.

"Who said I was even gonna let you out of my bed tomorrow?"

REILLY COULDN'T BELIEVE BRADY WAS STANDING ON her front porch inviting her to his house.

"You're gonna give me whiplash, Mr. McCord," she mumbled, hating herself for considering this. The man had rejected her not an hour earlier because he was being all noble and shit.

Another loud rumble of laughter sounded from Tate's bedroom.

It honestly gave her the willies to think about what those two were doing in there.

"Fine," she blurted. "But only so I don't have to listen to them."

Brady grinned. "That's good enough for me."

"I need a minute to change."

His gaze raked down her body slowly. "No need. I'll be takin' it off you anyway."

Ah, jeez. That tingling sensation had returned, only this time it was set to stun.

She heard voices coming from Tate's room. Did she want to risk Donovan coming out and finding Brady here? If he did, there was no doubt in her mind Brady would turn tail and run. And where would that leave her? Waiting? Wanting?

Fuck it.

"Fine," she told Brady, putting her hand on his chest and pushing him outside. "But I have to be back early to get dressed for work."

She didn't wait for him to respond, closing the door and pressing her fingers on the control panel to lock the door. She had her phone in her pocket, and that was all she really needed.

Brady took her hand and led her out to his fancy Cadillac. He opened the door for her, then waited until she climbed inside before closing it. She giggled when the cold leather chilled her legs, then buckled her seat belt while he walked around to the driver's side.

The car smelled like him. A light musky scent that reignited those damn tingles.

"Are you cold?" Brady asked as she was pulling her headphones from around her neck.

"A little," she admitted, feeling a bit nervous now that they were really doing this. It was one thing to be spontaneous about it, something else entirely to have to sit and wait to get to his house so he could ravish her.

Brady reached over and pressed a button on the dash. "Seat warmer."

Reilly grinned. "Not sure how much warmer it needs to get down there."

His slight inhale pleased her. She wasn't above teasing him.

He waited until they were off her street before he said, "How long have … uh … Donovan and Tate…?"

"Since tonight," she told him, shifting in her seat so she could look at him. "Why?"

"No reason."

"Tate's had a thing for him for a long time."

Brady nodded as though that made sense.

Unlike Tate, Donovan wasn't *flamboyantly* gay, as Tate liked to say. He was out and had been since Reilly was a kid, but she'd never known her brother to date a man like Tate. His tastes leaned toward men like him. Brooding alphas. Tate was the farthest thing from it, and that was probably why Reilly loved him so much.

Not that Tate and Donovan were dating. She hoped they were, of course. For Tate's sake. But she also knew that Tate was convinced that one night was all he needed with the big, brooding cowboy who'd struck his fancy a long time ago.

"Does it bother you?" she asked, more to make conversation than anything.

"What? Donovan and Tate?"

Reilly nodded.

"No. Should it?"

She shrugged. "You seem to have all these reservations about weird shit. Just thought I'd ask."

Brady shook his head and grinned. "I don't have reservations."

"My apologies. I guess when you said"—she lowered her voice to mimic his—"*'Donovan'll kill me,'* you were referring to something else."

"Reilly…"

"Don't get your panties in a twist, Mr. McCord," she teased. "I'm just givin' you shit."

He reached for her hand but not to link their fingers. Brady tugged on her arm until she leaned toward him. When she did, he pressed her hand to the hard ridge that was becoming best friends with his zipper.

"You keep callin' me that, and we're gonna have a problem."

To prove she wasn't scared of him, Reilly rubbed his erection through his jeans. "Doesn't feel like a problem to me, *Mr. McCord.*"

"Just wait, little girl."

Oh, man. Now *that* … that she could totally get behind. Reilly'd been on an age-gap kick for a while now, reading all the books she could get her hands on. The filthier, the better. And the ones with that whole daddy kink really did it for her. Not so much using the term daddy, but that authoritative dominant male thing revved her engine like nothing else.

Not that she wanted to tell Brady that. After all, he was the reason she had that particular fetish, and the last thing she wanted was to point out their age difference. He was already hung up on her being Donovan's little sister. He didn't need another excuse not to follow through.

Brady pressed his hand over hers, urging her to rub him harder. She leaned into him, resting her head on his arm as she ground her palm against his cock.

"I guess you haven't reached the age when you need that little blue pill, huh?"

Brady choked on a laugh, releasing her hand and shifting his arm around her. "Jesus, girl. You're gonna be the death of me."

A moment later, she was thinking the same thing about him because moving his arm hadn't been a casual gesture on his part. Proven when his hand slipped beneath her oversized sweatshirt, his palm sliding over her ribs, inching higher until he was cupping her breast. She was so glad she'd taken off her bra because ... man, his hand felt good on her bare skin.

Every cell in her body spiked in temperature. Her pussy throbbed, aching for more of his touch.

"I can take it off if you'd like," she offered, continuing to gently rub him through his jeans. "My shirt, I mean."

"Not a good idea. I'd like to get us to my house in one piece. Do it, and I'll be too distracted to drive."

Oh, he said the sweetest things.

"How distracted will you be if I do this?" she asked as she popped the button free on his jeans.

He inhaled sharply.

Reilly took that as a green light, so she slowly slid the zipper down, one tooth at a time.

His hand tightened on her breast when she scraped her nail along the silky boxers covering his cock.

"Fuck." He shifted in his seat, giving her more room to play. "Fair warning. Keep it up, and I will paddle your ass before the night's over."

"Promise?"

"So fucking much," he gasped when she tugged the waistband of his boxers down enough to free the thick, swollen head of his cock.

He was huge. Bigger than she'd anticipated. Bigger than her favorite dildo, even, and that thing was rather hefty.

"How far are we?" Reilly asked as she rubbed the bead of precum with her thumb.

"Fifteen minutes."

"You should hurry."

Nine

IF DONOVAN HAD EVER WANTED TO TAKE his time with someone, he couldn't remember it. With Tate, he realized that was the only way they'd survive it. And not simply because Donovan would split him in two if he fucked him the way he was tempted to. No. Tate was small, but he could handle him. Donovan would never underestimate this man.

Reaching between them, Donovan wrapped his fist around both their cocks, stroking slowly until Tate broke the kiss, gasping for breath as his eyes rolled back in his head. He admired the way Tate rocked his hips, fucking himself on Donovan's hand. He wasn't in a hurry, simply enjoying the sensation.

Donovan nipped his lower lip before he got too far away. "Put that sweet little mouth on my dick."

Tate's eyes opened, flashing with heat the same way they had when Donovan called him *little boy* a minute ago. It hadn't been intentional, but for some reason, their size difference was a complete turn-on for him. And he suspected it was for Tate, too.

Donovan grabbed one of Tate's pillows and balled it up beneath his head so he could stare down his body and watch as Tate began stroking him, his pale skin a stark contrast to Donovan's dark, blood-filled cock. The muscles in Tate's arms flexed and bunched as he massaged him, and when Tate licked his lips, Donovan's dick jerked in Tate's hand, causing Tate's gaze to dart to his face.

"That's what lookin' at you does to me," he admitted. "You make me fuckin' hard, Tate."

Tate's hand paused as he stroked him, his eyes glassy with lust.

"Suck it," Donovan said gruffly.

Tate leaned down, his breath fanning the head of Donovan's dick for a few seconds before his tongue slipped out to lap at the precum pooling on the tip. Donovan was riveted by the sight of Tate teasing him with light flicks and lingering caresses before finally wrapping his lips around the head. He sucked like he was using a straw before opening wide and taking more of him. Donovan watched as Tate took at least half of him into his mouth before he bobbed back up. Again and again, Tate made love to his cock with his mouth. It was unlike anything Donovan had ever felt before. He'd been with plenty of men, some who enjoyed sucking cock, some who only wanted to be sucked. Tate wasn't simply trying to please Donovan; he was savoring it.

For long minutes, he watched Tate, noting the way he was constantly looking up at Donovan.

"You've got a sweet fucking mouth," he said, wanting to reassure Tate that he was enjoying it. "Use your hand and take more of me."

Tate curled his fingers around the base of his shaft as he lowered his head, taking Donovan deep into his throat. He didn't gag because he took his time, swallowing when the head was lodged against his tonsils. It was fucking heaven.

When Tate licked his way down Donovan's shaft, shifting lower, Donovan planted his feet on the bed and spread his knees wide.

"Oh, yeah," he groaned when Tate licked his balls, gently laving at first before sucking one and then the other. Again and again, he was driving Donovan out of his fucking mind.

He was watching when Tate slipped his finger into his mouth and lubed it with spit. Then as he began to caress Donovan's asshole, lightly rimming him at first.

"Careful," Donovan warned.

"You don't like it?"

"Oh, I definitely do," he admitted. "But you're shredding my restraint. You might find yourself gettin' more than you're ready for."

Tate's blue eyes widened, but there wasn't a hint of fear on his face. He held Donovan's stare, daring him to do his worst, as he pushed his finger into him, fucking gently. It was so fucking good Donovan had to grip the base of his cock to keep from exploding before he was ready. He allowed him to play for another minute, but then his restraint snapped.

He lunged for Tate, grabbing him and shoving him face-first into the mattress as he covered him with his body, letting him feel every hard inch of him. Tate relaxed beneath him as Donovan pressed his chest to his back and slid his cock between Tate's tight little ass cheeks.

Oh, yeah. This was going to be fun.

"Are you scared now?"

Tate turned his head to the side, trying to reach Donovan's mouth. "No."

"Good. Now stay right where you are. Move, and I'll spank your ass before I fuck it."

Tate groaned, making Donovan grin.

"You like that, huh?" he asked as he got off the bed to retrieve the condom in his wallet and the small applicator-sized lubricant he kept on hand.

"Yes," Tate admitted.

"Good, boy," Donovan praised.

Tate remained where he was as he watched Donovan open the condom and roll it on before he twisted the tip of the lubricant and squeezed the contents in his hand. He generously coated his cock and his fingers before moving onto the bed behind Tate.

"Lift that sweet ass up," he said, smacking Tate gently.

Another groan as Tate got into position.

"Be easy," Tate said.

Donovan chuckled. "You think I'd impale you on my dick just like that?"

Tate grunted.

"You're not ready for me yet," he said, gripping Tate's hips before leaning down and running his tongue along the crack of his ass, teasing his hole lightly at first.

"Oh, God, yes," Tate cried out, pushing his hips back when Donovan began teasing more urgently.

Reaching around, he gripped Tate's cock, letting him fuck his hand while he rimmed his hole, stirring the sensations in those sensitive nerve endings. When Tate's cock was rock hard, Donovan pushed one finger into his ass, fucking him slowly. He kept at it, letting Tate work himself into a frenzy, rocking his hips.

"More," Tate pleaded.

Donovan added another finger. He worked him then, stretching his tight hole by scissoring his fingers while continuing to massage his cock, getting him right where they both needed him to be.

"Donovan…"

"Tell me, baby," he growled softly.

"Fuck me. Please. Fuck me with your monster cock."

"You sure you're ready?" he asked, pushing three fingers into his asshole.

Tate groaned, his back arching as he tried to ram back against the intrusion. "Yes. I need you to … I need you to fuck me."

Donovan's cock kicked hard, eager to slide into the hot depths of Tate's body. He moved slowly, withdrawing his fingers before guiding his cock home.

"Bear down," Donovan told him as he pushed his hips forward, watching as his cock stretched Tate's hole.

Damn, that was pretty. He couldn't look away, admiring the way Tate's body slowly accepted him.

Tate grunted as he pushed back at the same time Donovan pushed forward, sinking in slow and deep. Donovan went slow but not too slow. Deep but not too deep. He rocked his hips, shallow thrusts as he worked Tate open, allowing him to take more of him.

"You're so fuckin' tight," Donovan rasped, holding Tate's hips still. He didn't want to hurt him. "Can you take more?"

"There's more?"

Donovan laughed. "You've taken half."

Tate chuckled and groaned, dropping his chest to the bed as he began fucking himself onto Donovan's cock.

"That's it," Donovan urged, resting on his heels as he pulled Tate back with him, giving him control for a moment. "Take more of me, little boy. Fuck that tight little ass on my dick."

While Tate controlled the pace and depth, Donovan reached under him, stroking Tate's cock firmly, pumping his hand up and down his shaft until Tate was panting and moaning.

"Fuck, that's pretty," Donovan told him, smacking Tate's ass. "The way your little hole stretches around me." He smacked him again. "This greedy little ass."

"Oh, God," Tate cried out. "Don't stop."

Donovan smacked his ass again. "Don't stop what? Stroking? Spanking? Or fucking?"

Tate grunted. "Donovan … please … more. Fuck me. Fuck me hard."

He tormented Tate for a few more seconds before he grabbed his hips and pushed in as deep as Tate's tight little body would allow. He fucked him with shallow strokes, gaining momentum until Tate's hole opened to allow him to sink all the way in.

"Oh, fuck yes," Donovan growled. "Oh, fuck, you feel good.

Only then did he fuck him. Watching as Tate's hands fisted the blankets and he begged for more.

"Donovan … please … I need to come. Please. Can I come?"

"I don't know, *can you?*"

"May I?" Tate amended. "May I come?"

Donovan rammed into him again and again, lightning sparking in his spine. This man turned him on in a way Donovan wasn't prepared for. He usually went all night, but Tate was asking so sweetly it was too hard to resist.

Tate reached underneath him, and Donovan watched his arm muscles flex and bunch as he jerked himself off.

"Come for me, baby," Donovan growled, impaling him on his cock, fucking him with blistering speed until he couldn't hold back. "Ah, fuck, Tate. Come for me."

Tate grunted and jerked under him, hissing as he came.

Donovan slammed into him one final time and drained his balls. He felt the orgasm through his entire body, which quite possibly was a first for him. He shuddered and growled, holding Tate's hips tightly until he was spent.

Only then did he fall to the side and grab Tate, pulling him back against him. He'd never been the cuddling type, but this … it felt right. More so than anything else ever had.

Ten

BRADY SHORTENED FIFTEEN MINUTES INTO TWELVE, AND it had taken every ounce of concentration to keep his eyes on the road and not focus on the way Reilly was playing with his dick. Thank God she hadn't put her mouth on him. If she had, there was a good chance he would've run off the road. As it was, her touch was wickedly perfect. Combine that with her sassy retorts and he wasn't sure how he'd survived this far.

He pulled down the driveway, forcing himself to keep driving rather than stop and beg her to suck him. He even managed to tap the button for the garage door and waited patiently for it to open. After that, he didn't remember much. Somehow, he managed to park, turn off the engine, and close the garage door.

"Don't move," he told Reilly as he got out.

He tucked his cock in his underwear but didn't bother fixing his jeans. They would be off soon. But first, he intended to return the favor, and he planned to do it before they stepped foot inside the house.

When he opened the door, Reilly was sitting primly in her seat, clearly taunting him since he told her not to move. Brady chuckled as he reached across her and unbuckled her seat belt, then shifted her knees toward him. Before she could get out, he spread her thighs and ran his hand up the inside of one, not stopping until his fingers slipped beneath the snug cotton of her shorts.

"Fuck," he groaned. "Where are your damn panties?"

"Hmm. I must've forgotten them," she said, spreading her legs wider as he dragged his finger between the seam of her pussy lips.

She was wet and hot, and he knew it didn't have a damn thing to do with the seat heater.

"Lean back," he urged because he simply couldn't wait.

Her eyes were hooded and glassy, but she managed to prop herself on one arm, leaning back as much as she could with the center console behind her. Brady set her foot on the door's armrest as he tugged her shorts to the side so he could admire her soft pink flesh.

"Brady…"

"Hmm?" He lifted his gaze to hers.

"Don't stop," she whispered. "Please."

He grinned. "When you ask so nicely…"

Leaning down, he licked her. He'd intended it to be a tease, to pay her back for what she'd done to him. But the moment her flavor hit his tongue, he knew he didn't have the restraint to stop. He lapped at her with his tongue, slowly at first, then more insistently as her soft hum became frantic whimpers. He wanted her to come on his face but not like this. He needed more room. He wanted to spread her out on his bed so he could feast on her for hours.

Reilly fisted his hair, holding him in place. "Brady…"

It took more effort than he thought he was capable of, but he managed to pull back. He didn't go far, grabbing her hand and tugging so she fell forward. When she did, he grabbed her around the hips, lifted her off her feet, and tossed her over his shoulder.

"What are you doing?" She giggled exuberantly and grabbed for the waistband of his jeans, holding on as he carried her into the house.

He bypassed the kitchen and the living room and went right for the stairs that led to the second-floor loft. He designed the house himself, the open concept allowing him to have a full view of nearly every room from upstairs. There was little privacy, but he didn't need it. He lived alone and preferred the openness. It was his sanctuary, his refuge. Reilly was the first woman he'd brought here, and he hadn't thought twice about it.

"I can walk, you know," she said as he reached the top of the stairs. "I'm too big for you to carry."

"You're *perfect* for me to carry," he corrected.

When he dropped her onto his bed, she quickly propped herself up on her elbows, staring at him as he tugged one of her slippers off and dropped it to the floor. He made quick work of the other, then reached for her shorts, dragging them down her long, toned legs.

"You have the most incredible legs," he said, sliding his hands up them as he pushed her legs back and wide, admiring the glistening pink flesh between them. "And the most beautiful pussy."

Reilly moaned low in her throat when he lowered his mouth to her and fucked her with his tongue.

"Brady..." She groaned long and low, pumping her hips, attempting to fuck herself on his tongue.

He licked his way to her clit, but not before sucking on the smooth, puffy lips. He teased the swollen nub with the tip of his tongue, and her leg muscles tensed as she cried out so sweetly. He couldn't get enough. He wanted to feast on her pussy for the rest of the night. Tomorrow he could succumb to the overwhelming urge to fuck her.

If only he had that sort of restraint. Her soft mewls and guttural moans were driving him out of his mind. He wanted her to scream for him. He wanted her to cry out his name while he pounded himself inside her.

When he sucked on her clit, Reilly's hips bucked. He savored her, lightly sucking, gently stroking with his tongue, working her into a frenzy one glorious minute at a time until he felt the delicate pulse against his lips. She was going to come and he was ready.

"Brady ... oh ... yes ... it feels so good..." Still propped up on her elbows, she arched her back and cried out, the sound ripping from her throat as her pussy gushed. He lapped at her sweetness until she grabbed his hair and pulled. She wasn't gentle, urging him onto the bed with her.

As he moved over her, she reached for the hem of his sweater, jerking it up, obviously eager to get him naked. He didn't stop her. Only helped when she started shoving at his jeans. Brady had to get off the bed to discard the rest of his clothes and watched with unabashed interest as she stripped her sweatshirt off, tossing it to the floor.

"Oh, Jesus," he muttered, admiring every mouthwatering inch of her. She was stunning. In a way no other woman would ever compare. Her breasts were large and firm, her waist narrow, her hips perfectly rounded to grip while he drove himself deep inside her.

He was sweating. Ogling her and breaking a sweat because she was that fucking hot. He didn't know which part of her he appreciated more, but as a whole, she was utter perfection. Brady wanted to spend days ... hell, *decades*, ravishing her in every way possible. She was so fucking beautiful, it hurt to look at her.

He stopped looking only long enough to grab a condom out of his nightstand. He tossed it on the bed beside her.

This time, when he crawled onto the bed, she sat up, cupping his face and bringing his lips to hers. She thrust her tongue in his mouth as she pulled him down with her. He nipped her lower lip to slow her down. He wasn't done. Not by a long shot.

"Can you taste yourself?" he whispered against her mouth.

She hummed.

"Your pussy is so fuckin' sweet." He smiled when she licked his lips. "I could feast on your pussy day and night."

She hummed again.

"Don't move," he instructed as he crawled over her, not stopping until he was straddling her waist, his knees pressed under her arms, his cock tucked between her fantastic tits.

Brady had dreamed about fucking her tits. The woman had a thing for wearing teeny, tiny bikinis when she was hanging out in her parents' swimming pool. At least when he was around. And every damn time he saw her, he thought about his cock sliding between the soft, pillowy mounds, her smooth skin caressing him.

"I need to fuck your tits," he said, more to himself than to her because he couldn't help it. He was right where he wanted to be.

He cupped her breasts as he fucked his cock between them, watching her as he did.

"Has anyone ever fucked them?"

Reilly shook her head, watching his cock as it tunneled between her flesh. She was so damn soft. Too soft. It felt too good. Knowing he was the first sent a rush of adrenaline into his blood.

"I could do this all fucking night," he said, wanting her to look up at him.

When she did, she smiled. "No one's stopping you, Mr. McCord."

Oh, she was a little devil minx. He'd never been into the older/younger kink, but he certainly saw the appeal. Especially when she called him that. There wasn't an ounce of respect in the formal moniker, only pure, unbridled lust. He fucking loved it.

"Hold them for me," he urged.

When Reilly cupped her breasts, squeezing them together, he focused on the pleasure of his cock sliding between them large, firm mounds. He teased her nipples with gentle swipes of his fingertips until they were hard little nubs. He then pinched both at the same time, watching her face, gauging her reaction.

"You like that?"

"Yes," she rasped.

He pinched them again, more firmly this time.

She gasped, her eyes closing. "Brady..."

"More?"

Reilly nodded.

This time, he pinched her nipples and held firm. "Let go."

She dropped her hands, and he held firm to her nipples as he rocked his hips, fucking between them.

"Oh, God!"

He had her repeat that several more times, loving the way her hips bucked up off the bed when the pleasure/pain rippled through her.

"Good girl," he whispered, admiring her. "Hold them again."

She cupped her breasts once more, and he released her nipples, gently massaging them to ease the sting.

"Open your mouth," he said, continuing to fuck her tits, pushing the head of his cock toward her lips.

She tilted her chin toward her chest, opening her mouth, allowing him to press the head against her tongue.

"I want that sassy mouth on me," he said, shifting forward, forgoing her tits for the moment.

Her head tilted back again, her eyes remained on his face as her lips parted.

"You teased me earlier. Now it's time to pay up."

She giggled, then licked the head of his cock.

"Fuck," he rasped, grabbing her hands and raising them over her head as she sucked him into her mouth. He held them to the bed as he leaned forward, pushing his cock inside the blessed warmth. Slowly. One inch at a time.

Reilly curled her fingers around his hands, holding tight. That silent gesture of trust tripped something inside him. He'd been worried Reilly wouldn't be able to handle him. Wouldn't be receptive to his brand of kink. He was an insatiable, aggressive, verbal lover. Always had been. To know he hadn't scared her thickened his blood.

"You like that," he said, his voice dropping an octave. "Me holding you down? Shoving my cock in your pretty little mouth?"

She nodded, sucking the head of his cock as he retreated.

"Suck me, Reilly. Show me how good that mouth is."

Her eyelashes fluttered as she took him deeper.

"So fuckin' sweet," he rambled, watching his cock tunnel past her lips. "Love my cock, baby."

Her tongue swirled around him as she took him in her mouth again and again.

"Oh, fuck, that feels good, sweet baby."

Brady stared down at her, watching as she took him deeper and deeper each time he pressed his hips forward.

"More," he said because he sensed she wanted his dominance.

She took more, lifting her head as he pushed into her mouth. He hissed when the head bumped the back of her throat.

He grunted as the pleasure slammed into him. "You're too fucking good at that."

And she was. He was lost in the sensation, but he wasn't ready to come yet. He wanted her wrapped around him when he did. He wanted to feel her tight pussy flutter around his dick when he let go.

He knew already that once wouldn't be enough. Hell, one night wasn't going to be enough.

But he figured it was better to hold off on telling her she'd be lucky if he ever let her leave. He wasn't sure if he was capable of letting her go.

Tomorrow.

Tomorrow he would break the news to this woman that all he wanted for Christmas this year and every year after was her.

REILLY WAS TAKEN ABACK BY HOW INCREDIBLY hot this encounter was. The way Brady controlled her, giving her pleasure simply by taking his own from her. His filthy words undid her. She'd never had a lover who knew how to take control like this, one whose vulgar language made her burn hotter, brighter. He was ruining her, second by second, because no one would ever compare to him.

"Aw, fuck, Reilly," he groaned, pulling his cock free from her mouth.

The next thing she knew, he was at her side, pulling her onto him. She rolled with him, covering him as their lips melded together, tongues seeking, hands searching. He was all hard muscle and smooth, warm skin. His hands were everywhere, heating her as they moved over her body with such intensity.

When one of his hands disappeared, it was so he could fumble for the condom, which was just out of reach. Reilly chuckled, pulling her mouth from his and taking care of retrieving it for him. She inched back as she ripped the package open with her teeth, then pulled the latex disk out.

Brady's eyes lingered on her face while she did the honor of covering him. She met his gaze as she rolled the condom down his impressive length, loving the way his lips parted as pleasure coursed through him.

Reilly remained in control, holding his stare as she guided him home. She gasped as she slid down on him, her hands landing on his chest so she could control the pace. Slow. So, unbearably slow because his eyes turned glassy, and she could see the heat churning in the dark brown depths.

No man had ever looked at her the way he was. No man had ever made her feel like she was the most beautiful woman in existence. She wasn't sure whether it was intentional on his part, but she would never forget this moment for as long as she lived. Because it was then that her love for him became a palpable thing. This wasn't merely sex. Not for her. She'd had that before. The only sex thing. Pleasure for the sake of pleasure. But this ... it was far more intense. The sensations were heightened because it wasn't merely physical. Every part of her—heart, body, soul—was alive to feel everything. She would keep pretending it was only physical so she didn't scare him off, but this was so much more.

This was everything.

"Oh, fuck," his head tipped back. "Your pussy's so fuckin' tight."

His cock filled her, stretched her while his vulgar words caused tremors to erupt.

Brady grabbed her hips and held her still once he was fully seated inside her. Reilly groaned. She wanted to move. She wanted to feel every inch of him inside her.

"Let me ride your cock," she pleaded, meeting his heated stare, holding it. "Let me, *Mr. McCord.*"

He groaned again, and his grip loosened on her hips, but he didn't drop his hands. Instead, he began guiding her. Forward, back. The momentum increased until she was lifting and lowering, fucking herself on him. He never let go, urging her up and jerking her down, giving her everything she needed.

When her legs grew weak, Brady rolled, his cock lodged deep inside her. And then she was beneath him, her leg propped up by his hand as he drilled her at an angle.

"Look at me," Brady growled roughly.

Reilly opened her eyes, searching his face, falling deeper and deeper every second. She prayed he couldn't see that this was so much more than what she'd pretended it to be, but not because she wanted it to be a secret. She wasn't willing to do anything that would make this stop. If he needed her to remain aloof about it, she would. Just as long as he never stopped fucking her.

"That's it, sweet baby," he said, leaning down so his mouth was near hers as he slowed his pace, a beautifully brutal thrust that morphed into an equally delectable retreat.

"Brady…"

He smiled. "Let it feel good."

"It does … too good."

"Never. It only gets better."

He was right. It did.

Brady punched his hips forward, slamming into her. Reilly cried out, dragging her nails down his back as ecstasy flooded her system.

"Do it again."

He slammed in again.

"Oh, yesssss."

Again.

"Brady…"

Again.

"Oh, God … I'm so close."

"Yeah?"

She nodded, holding on as he rocked her into sweet oblivion, shaking her body with every punishing thrust of his hips. It was perfection.

"I want to feel you come," he whispered, his eyes peering into hers, seeing deep into her soul. "Come for me, Reilly. Come all over my cock."

She gasped and moaned as he took her right to the precipice, then let her drift there for several seconds before he drove her right over the cliff. Reilly cried out as the orgasm ripped through her entire being. She felt it everywhere, radiating from her core and out through her fingers and toes.

"You're so fucking beautiful," he growled as he stilled, his hips jerking as he came with her.

Eleven

Christmas Eve, Sunday, December 24th

TATE WOKE UP THE NEXT MORNING EARLY.

Far too early for anyone to be awake. Evidently, that included Donovan, who was sleeping soundly beside him.

He was tempted to pinch himself to see if he was still asleep because this ... it was some sort of Christmas miracle because the absolute last thing he expected was to find Donovan still there the morning after. Hell, it had been a leap to think the man would even sleep with him at all.

Tate slipped out of bed as quietly as possible, careful not to disturb Donovan. He tiptoed across the room, stopping twice to ensure he didn't so much as breathe loud enough to wake the man. When he reached the bedroom door, he opened it just enough to slip out of the room.

From there, he was a Formula 1 driver speeding around every corner of the house as he used the bathroom, found clothes, dressed, and slipped out of the house in record time.

He had to do some creative maneuvering to get his car out because Donovan had blocked him in. Thankfully, they had plenty of land, so he simply did a U-turn around the barn and came out the other side. If Reilly's parents happened to be watching out their back window, they were likely wondering what the hell was wrong with him.

Nothing.

Absolutely nothing was wrong.

Last night had been the most incredible night of his life. He doubted there was a man alive who could possibly top that, and Tate wondered if he would even bother trying in the future. There was a good chance he could remain celibate for the rest of his life and live off the memories alone.

So why was he leaving? Simple. He didn't want to be left.

Yeah, it was probably a dick move to leave Donovan in his bed, sound asleep. There was a chance—remote though it was—that he could've woken Donovan up, enjoy some more of that exquisite fucking he'd received last night before the day got started. But where would that leave him? Tate did not want to be the one left behind the morning after. He wasn't sure he would survive it.

He'd told Donovan last night that he didn't want any promises, and the man hadn't made him any. After that incredible encounter, Donovan hadn't so much as moved. Tate had been the one to remove the condom and toss it into the trash. Tate had been the one to clean them both up, to strip the comforter off the bed and replace it with one of the enormous blankets Reilly kept by the couch. And Tate had been the one to crawl back in bed with Donovan only to find himself wrapped in the man's arms as soon as he was horizontal.

To say it had been the perfect night was a complete understatement.

But there was a drastic difference between night and the morning after. With the light of day came regret, and Tate wasn't sticking around for Donovan to sprinkle a few on his perfect night sundae. He told Donovan last night that he didn't need promises and he hadn't been lying.

Of course, that was before Donovan gave him the most incredible night of his life. Before Tate had realized just how in love with Donovan he was. For years, he'd been lusting after the man, but his feelings for Donovan had started about the same time as his physical attraction. More specifically, back when Tate was seventeen and his mother kicked him out of her house because she couldn't condone Tate's "lifestyle".

As though being gay was a fucking lifestyle.

Reilly and her family had taken him in, brought him into their home, and insisted he stay there for as long as he needed to. At the time, Reilly was the only one of Owen and Deborah's kids who still lived at home, so it hadn't been too much of an inconvenience. Because they were seniors in high school, Tate hadn't put up a fight, figuring he could easily ride it out until he graduated.

For the first week, Tate had been in denial. He'd been hurt but also angry at his mother, so he rode out the pain in a haze of fury. By the second week, he felt abandoned and unwanted.

That was when Donovan came to his rescue.

Tate knew Reilly was the one who called him because Donovan was gay, and she knew if anyone could help him find his footing in the world, it was him. And it worked. Donovan had told him that it wasn't Tate's job to make people see clearly, that he couldn't take responsibility for anyone else's shame. Yeah, Tate had looked up to the guy, and he'd respected him, but he'd also been a little in love with him, too. That had sealed it for him, though. Tate had appreciated that Donovan would take the time to help him through the rough patch. After that, Donovan never harped on it, never acted as though he'd done anything at all, in fact. The man was simply there for the people he cared about, and Tate knew he always would be.

So, yeah, Tate had hoped that one day Donovan might look at him as something other than his little sister's best friend. Last night he had. And last night was perfect. Tate didn't want to do anything that would tarnish his memories of it, so here he was, in his car, driving around Coyote Ridge so he didn't have to be the one who was left this morning.

Donovan would get over it. Of that, Tate was certain.

As for his own heart … only time would tell.

DONOVAN WOKE UP AND INSTANTLY REACHED FOR Tate, only to find an empty place and a cold pillow.

He opened his eyes and looked around, listening for sounds coming from another part of the house. He didn't hear anything, but he smiled anyway. He found it amusing that he was usually the one to slip out of bed in the middle of the night, and Tate Riggs was the one who had turned the tables on him.

That had never happened before.

Usually, the men he spent the night with ended up being clingy and not necessarily in a good way. Honestly, he had expected Tate to be the same, and for the first time, Donovan would've welcomed it. He couldn't explain what made Tate different, but he was.

Apparently, more than Donovan had realized.

Once fully awake, he forced himself out of bed and pulled on his clothes before slipping out of the bedroom and heading for the bathroom. He did his business, then went searching for Tate, figuring maybe he could sweet talk the man into making some coffee. And if Tate wasn't willing, perhaps Reilly would be.

Granted, he wasn't exactly eager to have the conversation with his sister. The one that involved him telling her that he was interested in Tate, and no, he didn't know where this was going, but he was certainly willing to find out. There was no telling how Reilly would react. Not badly. He knew that much. But he could practically see his kid sister dancing around the living room, singing to the rafters about how happy she was.

No, he definitely wasn't ready for that.

Because the barn was basically one large room, except for the two bedrooms and the bathroom, it didn't take long to figure out that he was the only one there.

The house was empty.

Completely.

Reilly's bedroom door was open, but she wasn't in there.

Without putting on his boots, he walked outside and looked in the driveway. Sure enough, Tate's Mustang was gone. Reilly's truck was there, though, so where the hell was she? Did she leave with Tate?

"Fuck," he grumbled as he went back inside.

He pulled on his boots and grabbed his coat, feeling his frustration grow with every passing minute. He locked the front door with the press of his fingers on the keypad and pulled out his cell phone as he was walking to his truck.

He had Tate's phone number because he'd used it a few times to find Reilly. Now, as he stared at it, he wasn't sure what he was supposed to say to the man. He decided he wouldn't say anything. Not until they were face to face and he could confront him the right way. Why the fuck would Tate feel the need to disappear like that?

As he drove home to shower, Donovan thought about all the times the situation had been reversed. He'd always been clear about his intentions with the men he spent time with, so he didn't risk getting irate phone calls. That hadn't stopped a few of them from getting pissed anyway, but most were okay with temporary, so Donovan hadn't really thought about it much.

He could admit one thing: he didn't like being the one left behind. Not even a little.

Twelve

BRADY WOKE UP WITH A SMILE ON his face. He wasn't sure that had ever happened before.

Not specifically the smile. He wasn't nearly as grumpy as Reilly used to tease him about. Quiet was a better adjective. He internalized things these days rather than sharing them with everyone. That didn't mean he wasn't happy. Then again, until last night, he wasn't sure he had been. In fact, he wasn't sure he'd been feeling much of anything.

Now he was feeling everything.

So much he couldn't contain the smile or the lightness that came with it. As though something had been lifted off his chest, and he was no longer struggling to breathe. Reilly did that to him. She brought him back to life after he'd been stumbling around in the dark for so long.

Had that ever happened? Probably, at some point. But this felt different. *He* felt different.

Last night, after he'd cleaned up, Brady had come back to bed to find Reilly drifting off, worn out from their incredible lovemaking. At least, that was what he'd told himself as he'd crawled into bed beside her. As though she'd sensed his presence, she had curled up beside him, her head on his chest, her arm across his torso. They'd fallen asleep like that—cuddling. And Brady knew for a fact that no one had ever cuddled with him. The women he'd been with, including his ex-wife, had wanted to sleep on their own sides of the bed. Brady preferred intimacy, so the fact Reilly had slept in his arms had resulted in him getting the best sleep he'd ever had.

Okay, fine. Maybe he was overdoing it with the mushy shit this morning, but he didn't think so.

Glancing over at the clock, he saw that it was almost nine. It explained why Reilly wasn't in bed with him. He knew she opened the store at nine on Sundays, and with his luck, she had called an Uber rather than wake him up. He hoped not. He would gladly drive her into town, but first, he wanted to spend a few more minutes with her naked beneath him.

He listened for sounds she was still in the house, but he heard nothing. She wasn't banging around the kitchen, and there was no water running in the bathroom.

"Damn it," he grumbled as he forced himself out of bed.

He grabbed his boxers, pulling them on before padding through the bathroom. Empty. He did his business, then went downstairs, confirming his disappointment. She was gone.

For shits and giggles, he opened the door to the garage and stared at ... nothing. Like literally.

Now *that* was new.

For some reason, the fact that his Escalade was missing made him laugh out loud. So loud it rang through the house, which only made him laugh harder.

Reilly had stolen his car.

That girl.

He snorted, closed the door, then went back upstairs to get his phone. He saw he had a text message from her.

—I didn't want to wake you, so I stole your ride. Don't be mad. I'll make it up to you. Promise.

Mad? How could he possibly be mad? She was fucking adorable.

And yeah, Brady realized he was in deep. In all fairness, he knew that before what happened last night. Before he'd had the pleasure of her body. Now that he had, there was simply no way to deny it.

Which meant he needed to talk to Donovan. Brady had to come clean with his best friend before Donovan found out from someone else. It was almost guaranteed that someone would notice Reilly driving his SUV. It was only a matter of time before the grapevine got wind of it, and rumors started running rampant through town.

But first, he couldn't shake the idea of going to the General Store and telling Reilly good morning the right way. He missed her, and he honestly didn't want to start the day without seeing her beautiful face.

Yeah, he was in deep.

Half an hour later, after he showered and called an Uber, Brady was walking into the store, a smile on his face.

"Merry, happy, Chrismukkah!" Reilly greeted before turning around to see who was there.

Brady waited at the door, wanting to gauge her reaction. He wasn't sure how she felt about what happened last night.

She started to turn. "What can I—" Her sentence cut off as a radiant smile formed. "Good morning, *Mr. McCord.*"

The way she said that—all breathy and shit—really got his engine revving.

"Is it?" he asked, approaching slowly. "A good morning?"

He saw her hesitation. "I don't know. Is it?"

Brady didn't miss this part of the game. He hated not knowing where he stood or worried she felt the same. He'd done it too many times in his life, and he wanted this to be the last time.

"For me, it is," he said, ensuring she saw his sincerity. "The best in a long damn time."

Her smile returned. "I'm very happy to hear that."

Brady moved closer, skimming the store, curious whether Donovan was there. He no longer worked there with any sort of regularity, but he was known to come in and deal with other business. He claimed it was to keep Reilly company, but Brady knew her brother was protective of her. He worried about her being there alone.

"He's not here," Reilly said, obviously realizing who he was looking for.

"Do you know where he is?"

"If you're worried he's gonna walk in and catch—"

He put his hand over her mouth, silencing her. "I'm not worried."

She looked skeptical, and he couldn't blame her.

He lowered his hand and put it on her hip. "What is this, Reilly? This thing between us?"

Reilly moved closer, holding his gaze. "What do you want it to be?"

"Real," he said simply. "I want it to be real."

"Last night was real."

"It was," he agreed. "And the way I felt this morning was real."

She smirked. "Before or after you realized I stole your car?"

Brady chuckled. "Both."

Her voice lowered to a raspy whisper. "Are you gonna punish me, Mr. McCord?"

His cock twitched. "Most definitely."

"Promise?"

He wanted to promise a lot of things, but Brady settled for kissing her. It started sweet but went nuclear within a second. He wasn't sure where he found the willpower, but he managed to slow things down before he dragged her to the back room simply so he could bury himself inside her one more time.

"Is it real for you, Reilly?"

Her gaze searched his face. "I don't know what that means."

He held her hips. "Is it real enough for me to talk to your brother?"

Her eyebrows jumped. "You want to tell Donovan about us? Or you want to ask him for permission?"

Brady could've played the question game for half an hour, turning it around on her, but he decided to go with the truth.

"I want to *tell* him. I want to tell your whole family, Reilly."

"Really?" Her smile flashed merry and bright. "You're not worried it's too fast?"

"Are you?"

"Nope," she said with a loud pop on the "p".

"Then you're okay with it?"

"What if Donovan gets mad?" She tilted her head. "Just playin' devil's advocate."

"He'll get over it."

"Will he?"

Brady wasn't sure either, and yesterday, he had been worried about it. But everything changed last night, and Reilly had become his only concern. He wasn't lying. This was as real as it got for him, and now the only option was to tell Donovan and hope for the best. He figured if their friendship were as solid as he thought it was, Donovan would be happy for them. If not ... well, if not, then Brady would deal with that.

"If you want the same thing I do," Brady told her. "Then it won't matter."

He swore he saw tears in her eyes a second before she threw her arms around him. She didn't answer, but he could feel her smile against his neck.

"I'll take that as a yes."

She nodded, her chin digging into his skin.

Another round of relief swept through him as he held her.

But the next words out of her mouth made him go stone still.

FORTY-FIVE MINUTES AFTER HE'D LEFT TATE'S bed, after he showered and downed two cups of coffee at his house, Donovan got in his truck and headed for the store. He figured Reilly would be in, and if he was lucky, that was where Tate was hiding. Confronting the man was the only thing he could think about right now, and he intended to do so before too much time had passed.

Not once did he stop to think about why he wanted to confront him, though. If he had, Donovan would've realized his emotions were getting the best of him. Because last night ... last night hadn't been about sex. It hadn't been about using Tate's body in the best way possible.

Sure, the sex had been off-the-charts incredible, and he'd certainly used Tate's body, though not nearly as much as he wanted to. However, it was more than the too-short time he'd spent buried inside Tate. So much more.

Donovan made it to the General Store in less than ten minutes. As he walked toward it, he skimmed every car parked nearby. There weren't that many. It was relatively early on Christmas Eve, not to mention a Sunday, so most people were likely at home in their beds or getting ready for church. They weren't traipsing through town hunting for the man they'd spent the night with.

Yeah, it was a first for him too. So fucking what.

Not seeing Tate's car anywhere, Donovan parked in the lot behind the shopping center, next to Brady's SUV. Had he been thinking straight, perhaps he would've wondered why Brady was up this early. As it was, he didn't care.

He marched around the front of the building, grabbed the door, and flung it open, hoping to find Tate inside.

REILLY WAS NEAR TEARS, TOO HAPPY FOR words.

But as much as she wanted to remain like this for the rest of the day, she couldn't.

"I hope you mean that, Mr. McCord," Reilly whispered near his ear. "Because my brother's about to … open … the … door."

Reilly released him and took a step back. She met his gaze and tried to see if he'd been messing with her. Brady was still smiling, and her heart skipped a beat or two.

"Hey," Donovan grumbled. "You seen Tate?"

Reilly turned toward her brother. "Happy Christmas Eve to you, too, D."

Donovan waved her off, and she sensed he was wanting an answer.

"No. I haven't seen him yet. He's supposed to come by, though. Why?"

"I need to talk to him."

Well, at least Donovan didn't blow off her question as he usually would. Reilly figured he didn't know she knew that he was at her house last night, locked up in Tate's room with him.

And since he wasn't mentioning it, she had to think he didn't realize she'd left at some point, either. Or that she hadn't come back. Then again, her truck would be in the driveway, and he could've thought she was hiding out in her room. Unless he looked. Since she left her door open last night, there was a good chance he did. He would've passed right by it on the way to the door.

But he'd come in looking for Tate, not her. That was a good sign, right? Well, considering, anyway. Since Tate should've been with Donovan, if Donovan had actually stayed the night, the man wouldn't need to search for him. So, how had he lost him in the first place?

Hmm. This was somewhat of a conundrum.

Donovan and Tate.

Reilly and Brady.

Donovan clearly didn't want to talk to her about Tate, but he wanted to find Tate. Again, good news.

And she wasn't sure he was ready to hear about her and Brady.

Whatever were they to do?

"Hey, man," Brady said to Donovan. "You wanna grab some breakfast?"

Donovan nodded even as he turned to look out the window.

Wow.

Reilly wasn't sure she'd ever seen him like this. What exactly happened last night? She wanted to ask, but something told her to hold off. Donovan seemed somewhat fragile, and to be fair, that was the first time in her life that she'd ever seen him that way.

"I'll be back before you close," Brady said, his voice low. "I'll drive you home."

Reilly nodded, then watched as Brady steered her brother out of the store and down the sidewalk.

Hmm. If she could be a fly on the wall.

Thirteen

TWENTY MINUTES AFTER BRADY AND DONOVAN LEFT, Reilly was
sitting on the counter, playing a game on her cell phone, when the
bells over the door jingled. She looked up to see Tate wearing what
was definitely the ugliest Christmas sweater in the history of
Christmas sweaters. Yeah, they had insisted they were wearing them
this year, but she thought for sure they'd have a reason to do so. A
random trip into town didn't seem to warrant it.

"Hey," he greeted, a cheerful gleam in his blue eyes.

Only that cheerful gleam wasn't exactly real. Or rather, it wasn't
truthful. He was pretending he was happy. Why? Did it have
something to do with Donovan?

"Hi," she said equally cheerfully as she assessed him a little more.
"What's up?"

Tate shrugged and brushed a lock of hair out of his face. "Just
came by to see if you needed help."

Yeah, he was hiding something all right, but he didn't look
distraught the way Donovan had a short time ago. She wasn't sure
that was a good thing, though.

"You wanted to work on your day off? Really?"

"Of course."

"Yeah?" She didn't believe him.

Tate nodded at the same time he said, "No."

Reilly laughed, and Tate's smile grew wider and wider.

"You weren't home last night," he said.

"I was there long enough to hear things that made me want to gouge my eardrums out."

His eyes widened. "Really?"

"Oh, yeah." She hopped down from the counter. "Even my headphones didn't drown out your—"

"Don't," he shouted with a laugh. "I'm so sorry."

"Don't be." She met his gaze. "I left when Brady showed up."

"Showed up?"

Reilly took a moment to explain what had happened at the gingerbread house.

"What is it with those two runnin' with their tails between their legs?" Tate asked.

Since it was obviously rhetorical, Reilly didn't respond.

"And then he stopped by the house," she added.

"And took you to his," Tate noted.

"Yep."

"How was it?"

"Incredible."

"And you're still smiling today, so that's good."

"I kinda stole his car so I could get to work." She lifted one foot, showing him she was still wearing her slippers because she didn't have shoes. Luckily, she kept a spare pair of yoga pants and a sweater in the store for the rare times she needed them for an actual yoga class. "He came by."

"And...?"

Reilly shrugged. She wasn't really ready to talk about it. Not until she knew for sure where things were going with Brady. Based on their conversation earlier, she got the feeling this was moving even faster than she'd hoped for. She certainly wasn't opposed to it because she'd been in love with the man for so long, it felt like they'd been doing this dance for ages.

"He seemed happy," she admitted, pausing for a beat before adding, "And then Donovan showed up."

Tate tried to play it off, but she saw right through him.

"Showed up lookin' for you," she said, raising her eyebrows, letting Tate know she had a lot of questions.

His head snapped toward her. "Me?"

"Filler words won't work on me, and you know it."

"What?"

"Stop playin' dumb. He came in lookin' for you. If you want my opinion, he didn't look happy." When he didn't say anything, she tacked on, "Did something happen?" Reilly held up a hand. "And I don't want specifics about last night. I mean … this mornin'?"

"I don't know," Tate said, chewing on his lower lip as he diverted his gaze. "Donovan was asleep in my bed when I left."

"You *left* him there?"

Tate nodded.

That explained the ugly sweater. It had been in the living room from when they pulled them out while decorating the Christmas tree weeks ago. He likely grabbed it before he ran out.

"Where'd you go?"

"For a drive."

Reilly waited for more. There had to be more.

"I didn't want to watch him walk away, okay?" Tate said softly. "I figured it'd be best if I wasn't there. That way, it wasn't weird for him."

And *that* certainly explained the forlorn expression on her brother's face earlier. He was out of sorts. Why wouldn't he be? She sincerely doubted that had ever happened to Donovan before. He was the one who walked away, never in reverse.

"So what now?"

Tate wouldn't look at her. "I don't know."

"Based on earlier, I think he's gonna track you down," she warned him. "Are you gonna talk to him if he does?"

A small smile formed on Tate's mouth, but it seemed bittersweet. "Maybe."

DONOVAN HAD COME LOOKING FOR HIM.

Tate wasn't sure how to feel about that.

Well, aside from the giddy tidal wave that was currently threatening to split him in half.

It had started just before he'd gotten to the store. During his time-wasting road trip this morning, he'd had plenty of time to reflect on last night, but it wasn't until he was heading here to talk to Reilly that he permitted himself to be happy about what happened. To not dwell on the *what might've beens* and to focus on carrying that exquisite memory with him for all time.

It was the reason he'd been smiling when he walked into the store to find Reilly sitting on the counter, her legs dangling over the side as she played on her phone.

But to learn that Donovan had come here looking for him ... maybe he wasn't on Santa's naughty list after all.

Fourteen

DONOVAN DIDN'T WANT FOOD, AND HE DIDN'T need more coffee, but he agreed to breakfast with Brady to get his mind off Tate.

At least for a few minutes.

He'd been thinking about the man—or rather, *obsessing*—since he woke up. He needed a break so he could calm down and come up with a rational plan to confront him rather than hunting him down, stripping him, and fucking him into submission. Sure, he *liked* the idea of doing it that way, but he wasn't a caveman, and he was trying to remember that.

And he also might've come because he'd seen Reilly hugging Brady, and he knew the man wanted to talk about her. At the very least, he owed Brady his attention. Even if he didn't care one way or the other that Brady and Reilly were interested in one another, his best friend didn't know that. As he'd said before, Brady was a stand-up guy, and he wouldn't do anything that might jeopardize their friendship.

"More coffee?" the waitress offered as she passed.

Donovan held his hand over the top of his cup. Any more caffeine and his brain was going to start buzzing.

"I need to talk to you about Reilly," Brady said after he'd picked at half the food on his plate.

Donovan tried to play it cool. "What's up?"

Brady squirmed, and it was almost enough to make Donovan laugh. He didn't. He was still too frustrated with Tate to laugh, but he appreciated how much this bothered Brady. It meant the man had good intentions. Otherwise, why would he give a shit at all what Donovan thought about it?

"I saw her last night in the park."

That was news to Donovan. "I thought you backed out."

"I did. Then Alyssa came over and forced me to go."

Now Donovan was paying attention. "Alyssa?"

"She was with Henry," Brady said, clearly sensing Donovan's concern with Brady spending time with his ex-wife.

Not that Donovan had a problem with her. He liked Alyssa. A lot, actually. The fallout between her and Brady had been a natural deterioration of the relationship. There was no one to blame. However, Donovan was concerned that Brady was interested in Reilly and spending time with Alyssa.

"So I went with them to appease her," Brady continued. "When we got there, I let them do their thing and went lookin' for you."

Donovan waited for him to continue.

"Reilly intercepted me."

He tried not to smile, but he couldn't help it. "Intercepted? So you're tellin' me she tracked you down?"

"No. I mean, yes, but no." Brady exhaled.

"Spit it out, Brady."

Donovan drained what was left in his cup and watched the man who, in his heart, was as much a brother to him as Stone and CJ as he fought some sort of internal battle.

When Brady finally met his gaze, there was a steely determination in his eyes. "I kissed her."

"And...?"

"That's not enough?"

Donovan leaned back and regarded his best friend. "I don't know. You tell me. You kissed her. Then what? You went off on your merry way?"

"No." Brady shook his head. "Yeah. At first." He sighed. "I told her I couldn't betray you like that."

He could practically hear that conversation in his head. Donovan knew Reilly, so he knew his baby sister wouldn't have let Brady get away with an excuse like that.

"Did she put you in your place?"

Brady's lips twitched and a smile formed. "Total smackdown."

"Reilly's good at that."

"Better than you know." Brady took another deep breath and looked him in the eye. "She walked away, and I let her. But when I left the park, I didn't go home. I went to her place."

Donovan tried to hide his reaction. If Brady had gone to Reilly and Tate's last night, he would've known Donovan was there.

Brady nodded as though he could read Donovan's mind. "Yeah. She was wearin' headphones, D." He grinned. "Tryin' to drown you out."

"Fuck," he groaned, leaning forward and resting his elbows on the table.

"I talked her into comin' home with me," Brady tacked on quickly.

Donovan lifted his head, slowly meeting Brady's gaze. Although he'd been indifferent to Brady and Reilly liking one another, his best friend taking his baby sister home wasn't something he'd considered. Not completely. He trusted Brady with his sister's life, but he wasn't sure he trusted the man with her heart. Reilly deserved a man who would—

"I'm in love with her, D."

The admission came swiftly and with enough power to push Donovan back in his seat. His previous train of thought completely derailed. Suddenly, he no longer felt the urge to string Brady up by the balls. In fact, he wanted to ask when the wedding was.

However, he wasn't above letting Brady sweat for a minute.

WHEN BRADY THOUGHT ABOUT TELLING DONOVAN THAT he was in love with Reilly, he didn't quite expect … this.

"It's about damn time," Donovan said, holding his gaze as a small smile tugged the corner of his lip.

Brady was stunned for a moment. *It's about damn time?* Seriously? That was the response he was going with?

111

"*That's* what you have to say? I tell you I'm *in love* with your baby sister, and you don't want to pound my face in?"

"For one, she's not a baby anymore, and I trust that if she wants to be with you, she has her reasons."

Brady cocked his head. "And you're teasin' me. Are you feelin' okay?"

"About this? Yeah, I'm good," Donovan replied. "You think I haven't noticed the way you look at her?"

Honestly, Brady thought he'd done a damn good job of hiding it, so no, he hadn't thought that.

Not for the first time since they sat down, Donovan's attention shifted out the window. "Honestly, I'm happy for you."

Brady took a sip of his coffee and stared at his best friend. Clearly, something else was on his mind. Something that made this conversation much simpler than it would've been otherwise. And if he had to guess, that something was Tate Riggs.

It took a minute, but Donovan looked at him again. "Hurt her and I'll break both your legs."

Brady grinned. "That's more like it." He set his coffee mug down. "So you wanna tell me what happened with you and Tate last night?"

Donovan's head snapped around so fast that Brady sat back and held up his hands in mock surrender.

"Hey, if you wanna pretend it's a secret, go for it." He lowered his hands and leaned in, resting his arm on the table. "But I know you were there. Your truck was out front. And like I said, Reilly was tryin' to drown out the noise with her headphones."

"Fuck." Donovan thrust his hand through his hair. "I didn't want her to find out like that."

Brady leaned forward. "Did you think you could keep it from her?"

Donovan shook his head. He opened his mouth but closed it just as quickly.

"So what happened?" Brady forged on. "And I'm not talkin' about details. I mean ... today."

"What're you talkin' about?"

Brady rolled his eyes. "Come on, D. I've known you damn near your whole life. You might not be the most pleasant guy to be around sometimes, but usually you've got a reason for gettin' pissed off."

Donovan leaned forward and sighed. "I'm not pissed. Okay, maybe a little. Fuckin' Tate," he muttered. "He was gone when I woke up."

"Like gone from the bed? Or…?"

"Gone from the house," Donovan said, staring into his nearly empty coffee cup.

Whoa.

Brady didn't mean to, but he laughed.

"Seriously?" Donovan shook his head. "You find amusement in my pain."

"Sorry," Brady blurted. "I just never thought there'd be a man with balls big enough to walk away from you. Damn sure didn't see it bein' little Tate Riggs."

Donovan rolled his eyes. "I wasn't expectin' it, that's all."

"That's not all," Brady said, sobering. "It's real for you. You can admit it."

He knew that like he knew his own name. Donovan didn't get pissy over the guys he was seeing. Hell, for the most part, he shrugged them off as though he could take them or leave them. This was quite possibly the first time Brady had seen him so twisted. Not since … a lifetime ago.

Donovan met his stare. "Yeah. It's real. At least I thought it was."

Brady didn't like the fact that was in the past tense. Although he wasn't sure when this came to be, Brady didn't want Donovan to give up too quickly.

"What're you gonna do about it?"

"Fuck if I know."

Donovan appeared sincerely stumped by the turn of events. Which was probably a good thing. Someone needed to shake up the man's life. Who would've thought it would be little Tate Riggs? And he meant that with the utmost sincerity. He liked Tate. Hell, the guy made him laugh all the damn time, especially when he got on his kick and started calling everyone sweetie.

Brady took a sip of his coffee and stared at his best friend. Yeah. He could definitely see Donovan with Tate. Complete opposites. But like they say, opposites attract, and as far as Brady was concerned, those two would be good for each other.

Of course, he never thought he would be thinking that. Then again, he'd never expected to spend a night with Reilly, so maybe they were in some alternate universe, and tomorrow they would wake up to find it was Christmas, and the past couple of days had been a dream.

He hoped not.

Brady's cell phone chimed. He peered down at the screen.

—You can tell my brother Tate's here at the store. In case he wants to talk to him.

Brady grinned wide. Leave it to Reilly to play matchmaker.

"Tate's at the store," Brady told Donovan.

The man attempted to school his expression, but Brady had known him a long damn time. That news was important to Donovan, and it was taking tremendous effort for him to remain sitting there when he obviously preferred to be somewhere else.

Figuring he could do his friend a favor, Brady waved the waitress over.

"Could we get the check?"

She smiled and nodded before grabbing their plates and heading to the kitchen.

"Is it serious, D?" Brady asked, losing all pretense of teasing.

Donovan looked up at him. "It was certainly headin' that direction, yeah."

"Tate's a good guy," Brady told him, purposely not referring to him as a kid, which he'd always done before. "I'm sure he can explain."

"Oh, he will," Donovan said, tossing back the last swallow of his coffee like it was a shot of whiskey. "I'll make damn sure of it."

Brady believed him.

AFTER REILLY TEXTED BRADY THAT TATE WAS at the store, she couldn't take her eyes off the door.

She wasn't sure whether she was eager to find out if Brady told her brother about... well, she figured he couldn't tell him much because she wasn't sure she would classify what happened last night as the beginning of a relationship. Yeah, she wanted to, but that didn't mean Brady was on the same page.

Regardless, she was curious to find out if Brady owned up to it, but she was a little more excited to see if Donovan would confront Tate. She was hoping for both but for entirely different reasons. Reilly couldn't forget the look on Donovan's face when he came into the store asking where Tate was. He'd been a man on a mission, the complete opposite of Tate, who was attempting to play it cool.

"Oh, shit," she blurted when she saw Donovan and Brady walking in front of the window, heading for the door. "They're back."

Her brother yanked the door open and stormed inside. He skimmed the room, but his eyes moved right past her, which was a huge relief. Maybe it was a good thing something happened between him and Tate. That meant she wouldn't have to endure Donovan's protective big brother spiel.

Before she could ask how they were, Donovan said, "Y'all should go. Enjoy the day. I'll lock up in a bit."

Go? Seriously?

"Donovan—"

"Come on," Brady said, crooking his finger at her while gesturing toward the door with his other hand. "He'll keep it open all day, won't you, D?"

"Yep."

Oh, yeah. Sure. He sounded like he was going to handle the store. If Reilly were to guess, she would say Donovan hadn't heard a single word Brady said.

Then again, to be fair, she didn't really care. It was Christmas Eve, and it was Sunday. They wouldn't see much traffic. No one had come in yet, and the morning was mostly over. Plus, if anyone wanted to give her a choice between spending the day with Brady or working the register, she would pick Brady every single time.

Starting now.

Before she walked toward Brady, she looked at Tate. "You good?"

He barely spared her a glance long enough to nod before his attention shifted back to Donovan.

"Call me later," Reilly told him.

Another nod, but this time, he didn't even look at her.

Reilly took that as her cue and hurried out the door with Brady. She giggled when he took her hand and darted toward the side of the building. As soon as they turned the corner, Brady pulled her up short, pressing her against the rough wood siding.

She gasped in surprise as she stared up at him. "What's wrong?"

"Absolutely nothing," he said, leaning in and sealing his lips to hers.

Reilly relaxed into the kiss, running her hands up the front of his shirt beneath his coat.

"Come home with me," Brady said softly. "I want to get you into my bed and not let you out until next year."

She chuckled. "You realize that's not too far away, right?"

"I meant the year after next."

Reilly giggled and pulled back, staring up into Brady's too-handsome-for-words face. "Okay. But I need to go home and get a few things. I haven't showered yet."

Brady looked down at her. "Where'd you get the clothes?"

"I keep a spare set here for when I go to yoga."

As though he was only noticing for the first time, his attention shifted to her feet.

"Yeah," she told him. "I don't keep shoes, so I had to wear my slippers."

"Ah."

"And I should get my truck so I don't have to steal yours."

He kissed her sweetly. "I don't mind. It gives me more reason to punish you later."

A wave of heat slammed into her. "Promise?"

Fifteen

DONOVAN TRIED TO PLAY IT COOL, STANDING only a few feet inside the store when Reilly and Brady left. He cleared his throat twice before he could find his voice.

Perhaps that was why Tate was staring at him, wide-eyed and timid.

"If you even think about runnin', you should know my truck's blockin' your car." He took a few steps, wondering if Tate was going to hop down from the counter. "You won't get far."

Tate's gaze swung to the front windows as though he might be able to see behind the building.

Or maybe Tate was nervous because Donovan was moving closer, skirting the register counter, and coming to stand behind it. He stopped when he was less than a foot away, standing between Tate's legs.

"You left," Donovan accused, not waiting for him to look at him.

Those big blue eyes slowly shifted to his face, and Tate's shoulders lifted slightly. "I did."

"Why?" He cleared his throat. "Why'd you leave?"

Tate's forehead creased. "What else was I supposed to do?"

"Stay," Donovan blurted. Wasn't it fucking obvious?

"Why? So you could be the one to walk away?" Tate rolled his eyes. "No thanks."

Donovan couldn't believe what he was hearing. He was stunned speechless for a moment, but it didn't last long.

"What did I do that would've possibly led you to believe I would've slipped out in the middle of the goddamn night?"

Tate's eyes widened.

No, Donovan wasn't trying to hide his frustration with this situation. He was pissed. And yeah, he was a little hurt because he thought last night had been ... well, if not special, it had at least been different. For him, anyway.

"All of it," Tate whispered.

"All of *what?*"

"Everything," Tate said through gritted teeth. "You made promises you didn't intend to keep, Donovan."

He frowned, trying to recall what he'd said.

"Not with words," Tate added, clearly sensing Donovan's confusion. "With ... what you did. The way you..."

"The way I what? Fucked you?" Donovan put his hands on Tate's thighs. "Because I didn't treat you like a whore?"

"Yeah," Tate bit out.

Silence echoed for a moment as they stared at each other. Donovan wasn't sure what to say, wasn't sure why Tate would make those types of assumptions. History, maybe? Or did he think that little of Donovan?"

"Goddammit," Tate hissed. "You made me want things I know I can't have. Is that what you wanna hear?"

Donovan leaned closer. "What do you think you can't have?"

They continued to stare at each other, both of them seething. Donovan wasn't backing down from this. He wouldn't. It was too damn important.

"You," Tate hissed. "I can't have you."

"Says who?" he snapped, never breaking eye contact.

Tate sucked in a sharp breath but he didn't say anything.

"Last night..." Donovan swallowed, gathering his thoughts. "What happened last night ... that doesn't happen for me."

Tate's big blue eyes widened. "What doesn't?"

He closed the gap between them, sliding his hands to Tate's hips and pulling him to the edge of the counter.

Tate's eyes shifted away quickly, but then the bells over the door jingled. Donovan didn't move. He remained where he was.

"Morning," Tate greeted.

"Can you ... uh ... tell me if you have toilet paper?"

Tate looked at Donovan, so he answered with, "Back wall, bottom right."

"Thank you," the woman said.

"This is unprofessional," Tate whispered when the customer disappeared to the back of the store.

"I don't give a fuck." And he honestly didn't. He was not letting Tate get away from him again.

Donovan watched Tate so he knew when the woman was coming back.

"It's on the house," Donovan told her without looking back. "Merry Christmas."

Tate nodded and smiled. "Merry Christmas."

"Thanks. You, too."

The bells jingled again as the woman left. Donovan gripped Tate's chin, forcing him to meet his gaze again.

"It doesn't happen to me," he repeated, picking up where they'd left off. "And I dare you to tell me you don't know what I'm talkin' about."

Those blue eyes glittered as Tate stared back at him, but he didn't say a word.

"You felt it," Donovan said, his voice soft and low. "I know you did."

For the first time in his life, Donovan knew what it felt like to be completely vulnerable to someone. Because right now, right here, he was stripped bare.

Tate couldn't believe this was happening.

He couldn't believe the words coming out of Donovan's mouth. Was he saying…?

"Yeah," Tate admitted. "I felt it."

"But you're content with one night?"

"I can be," he said without thinking.

"Why?"

Tate held Donovan's stare and ignored the pounding of his heart. "If that's all I can have…"

"It's not," Donovan growled, his hands sliding up Tate's back as he pulled him closer. "Are you even listening?"

Damn right, he was. He simply wasn't understanding. This never happened. For as long as he'd lusted after this man, he figured one night was a fantasy. Never did he think he'd get that much. Now Donovan was telling him—

"You can have me," Donovan said, his voice low. "If you want me."

Tate was positive he was dreaming. Or perhaps he'd been cast in one of those Hallmark Christmas movies, and no one had told him.

"Tate?"

"Hmm?"

"But only if I can have all of you."

It took a second for him to realize he was cupping Donovan's face with both hands, staring at him.

Donovan canted his head. "Tell me what you want."

"You, Donovan. I want you."

A rough growl rumbled in Donovan's chest, and the next thing Tate knew, he was crushed against him in a bear hug, their lips pressed together as Donovan licked his way into Tate's mouth. The kiss was surprisingly gentle, considering how tightly Donovan was holding him.

Tate's hands shifted to Donovan's thick, corded neck, and he held on while their tongues danced, and his chest expanded with an emotion he hadn't felt in a really long time.

This time, when the bells over the door jingled, Donovan released him. He didn't step back immediately, though.

"I'm gonna lock that fuckin' door," he mumbled under his breath before turning around.

When Tate looked up, he grunted with disappointment. Ben was standing there, staring at them like he'd never seen two men kissing.

"You could've just told me," Ben said, his tone biting. "I wouldn't've wasted my time."

"Something tells me you don't waste a precious second, Ben. If you're not with one guy, you're with another." Tate huffed a laugh, but it lacked an ounce of mirth. "Hell, even when you're *with* one guy, you're with another."

"Can we help you with somethin'?" Donovan asked, stepping out from behind the counter.

"Kinda creepy that you were kissing your dad," Ben retorted, directing the statement at Tate.

"If he calls me daddy, it damn sure ain't for reasons you're thinkin', boy," Donovan said, his tone dark and dangerous.

"Whatever. I didn't wanna be here anyway. See you around, Tate."

"No, you won't," Donovan told him as he followed him toward the door. "He'll be otherwise preoccupied for the rest of his life."

Ben's eyes narrowed briefly before he rolled them and walked out the door.

Tate couldn't find his voice, and he couldn't wipe the grin off his face. He'd wanted to put Ben in his place for a long time, but he never got the courage to stand up to him. The fact that he did and Donovan supported him made him a bit giddy.

Of course, the whole *he'll be otherwise preoccupied for the rest of his life* part didn't hurt. He wanted to believe that. He wanted to jump on board the *Forever and Ever, Amen,* train, but he was hesitant.

When Donovan turned back to him, Tate said, "I'm not callin' you *daddy.*"

Donovan's eyebrow quirked. "Up to you, little boy. But I'm still gonna paddle your ass."

Tate's dick swelled, making his jeans uncomfortably tight. He wasn't sure if it was the *little boy* bit or the promise of a spanking that did it, but his body was definitely on board. Perhaps it was simply the gruff tone of Donovan's voice or the glimmer of promise that flashed in his green eyes. Whatever it was, Tate knew he'd never been turned on by anyone like this. He was attracted to this man in ways he hadn't realized he was capable of. He wanted him. But more importantly, Tate wanted to surrender to him.

Donovan turned back to the door and locked it before flipping the sign over that read:

WE'LL BE BACK IN 15 MINUTES.
(If It's Been That Long Already,
Read The Sign Again.)

121

Tate seriously doubted fifteen minutes would be long enough, but he wasn't going to bring it up. Not when Donovan was stalking him like that.

A nervous laugh escaped Tate when Donovan grabbed him by the wrist and dragged him toward the back of the store. As they passed the condom aisle, Tate grabbed a box of the extra-large ones and snagged a bottle of lube while he was at it. In front of him, Donovan let out a gruff laugh that made Tate's cock swell even more.

"You want me inside you, huh?" Donovan asked when he pulled him into the storage room and closed the door. It was a relatively large room that acted as both storage and a small break area, complete with a recliner and a television. Not to mention a lock, which Donovan flipped as soon as the door closed.

Tate stumbled when Donovan dragged him toward the recliner, then stopped abruptly. He spun around and grabbed Tate, crushing his mouth on his. It was all he could do to hold on and succumb to the onslaught. The man kissed as though he was supposed to feel it throughout his entire body. And he did. There was no doubt when Donovan kissed him, Tate felt him everywhere.

"Strip," Donovan commanded when he finally stepped back.

Tate hesitated, but when Donovan yanked off his boots and pulled his long-sleeve shirt over his head, he got with the program. Within seconds, they were both naked and the next thing he knew, Donovan was grabbing him around the waist as he fell into the recliner. Tate ended up in Donovan's lap, his back pressed to Donovan's massive chest.

Donovan's hand curled around his throat, pulling him back as he held him in place. "I want to feel you," he rasped against his neck before he began sucking the sensitive skin.

Tate rubbed his ass against Donovan's cock as he passed him the box of condoms. Tate shifted, giving Donovan room to maneuver. The man managed to cover himself with lightning speed and then lubed them both in a hurry before he gripped Tate's hips and urged him to his feet. Donovan didn't let him go far, though. He guided him back down, directly onto his cock.

Tate hissed as he felt the pressure, then sighed when Donovan's cock breached the tight ring of muscle.

Time slowed. Everything slowed as Donovan gently yet firmly pushed his cock deep inside, filling him, stretching him. Tate relaxed, giving himself to Donovan, letting him have control because the only thing he wanted was to feel.

"Fuck yes," Donovan whispered, his fingers digging into the flesh of Tate's hips as he pushed him off before pulling him back.

Tate steadied his feet and let Donovan do all the work, impaling him on his cock. He groaned and sighed, letting the pleasure consume him, listening to Donovan's deep, guttural growls as he took his time, building up to what would no doubt be a dramatic finish.

"Tomorrow," Donovan said, his voice strained. "When you wake up in my bed, you damn sure won't be runnin' away. Will you?"

Tate eased down on Donovan's cock again. "No."

"And the day after that?"

Tate wasn't sure Donovan realized what he was saying, but he was afraid to mention it. He didn't want this to end. Even if they scared him, he wanted Donovan's promises. He wanted to know that this was more than really good sex. He *needed* it to be more.

Donovan pulled him down hard, impaling him as deep as he could go. His arms banded around Tate's ribs as he nipped his earlobe.

"Answer me, little boy. Answer me, and I'll fuck you the way you need to be fucked."

Why that turned him on, he didn't know, but it did.

"No, I won't run," he told Donovan even as he put his feet in the chair on either side of Donovan's legs so he could lift himself up and drop down onto him again.

"Ever," Donovan groaned. "Oh, yeah. Fuck me, Tate. Ah, God, yes."

Tate fucked him, bouncing on his cock as much as the position allowed. Donovan assisted, lifting him until he took over, holding Tate a few inches off of him and ramming his hips up, fucking him deeper than he thought possible.

"Donovan … oh, God…" The position caused Donovan's cock to rub his prostate so perfectly. "Oh, fuck … Donovan, may I come?"

Donovan growled and nipped his shoulder. "Fuck yes."

Tate took it as permission, and his restraint snapped. Sparks shot up his spine as he came in a blinding rush, cum splashing all over his chest and stomach. He gasped when Donovan jerked him down one final time, his cock pulsing deep inside him.

Only when he was trying to catch his breath did Tate realize that was the first time he'd ever come without touching his cock.

Sixteen

After leaving the General Store, Brady drove Reilly home.

Since she was going to drive her truck, he left, but only once she promised him she would wait to shower until she was at his house. He hadn't given her much choice. Not that she would've denied him anyway. The thought of what he might do to her beneath warm water made her skin prickle with heat.

She packed a bag with a couple of things, including clothes she could wear to her parents' house for Christmas dinner tomorrow, then she got into her truck and headed to his house. She'd never been inside it until last night, but she'd seen it from the outside a few hundred times, passing it whenever she went to Donovan's house.

In a lot of ways, it was like her brother's. And like Donovan's, it stood out from the other houses in Coyote Ridge. Their small town consisted of primarily ranch-style homes and a few elaborate farmhouses that sat on plenty of acreage. This modern structure looked like it belonged beside a lake or maybe an ocean where the occupant could enjoy the view from all angles. Or, yes, the small, two-acre man-made pond that sat behind it and separated the three houses on each side that backed up to it.

The entire neighborhood, which consisted of only a dozen homes, had been built with the view in mind, and since there hadn't been one, Brady and Donovan had created one of their own. She recalled when they got the idea to build it. They'd spent months looking for the right parcel of land that would accommodate their vision. They'd been disappointed when they'd lost out on the land that Alluring Indulgence Resort ended up on, but a few months later, this became available. One half of the neighborhood was in Coyote Ridge—the half Donovan and Brady lived on—and the other half was in the neighboring town.

Each residence had two and a half acres of land, and the houses were positioned directly in the center of the lot. Brady had a three-car garage on one side, all with single doors. The rest of the house was made of glass, something she hadn't thought much of last night. Probably because it was dark out. But now, as the sun glinted off the windows, she couldn't help but smile.

As she was pulling into the circular driveway, Brady came out the front door—which was also made of glass. There was no porch, merely large concrete squares—roughly five feet by five feet—that covered the space between the driveway and the front door.

"I guess you don't have an issue with modesty," she said when he opened her door for her.

Brady looked up at the house. "It's not as transparent as you might think. You can see out fine, but it's got a special tint that doesn't allow you to see in."

"And you've tested that theory?" She was really curious because last night, when they'd been in his bed, there was a good chance his neighbors got a show.

"If you're asking whether I walk around naked when the neighbors are out, probably not."

"That's a shame."

"I'll gladly give it a go if you will, though."

Reilly giggled, then allowed Brady to take her bag as he led her to the house.

"Are you hungry?"

"I had a cereal bar when I got to the store."

"So that's a yes?"

"Didn't you have breakfast with Donovan?"

Brady shook his head. "We didn't eat much."

"In that case, I could eat."

"Would you like to shower while I cook?"

Reilly moved closer to him. "I was thinkin' maybe we could shower together."

Oh, how she loved the way his dark brown eyes heated.

"You never did tell me what Donovan said," she mentioned as he led the way up the stairs to the loft.

Brady stopped as soon as he was at the top and turned to look at her. "He said it's about time."

Her eyebrows practically shot into her hairline. "Are you kidding?"

"No." He laughed, a gruff sound of disbelief. "He did add that if I hurt you, he'll break both my legs."

Reilly didn't start walking when he did. She was still trying to process that. Not the breaking legs part. She'd expected no less.

Brady appeared again. "You comin'?"

"Did Donovan expect you and me to…" She threw up her hands. "I mean, why would he say that?"

Brady helped her by grabbing her wrist and tugging her up the last two stairs and into the bathroom. Unlike the rest of the house, Brady had designed it to be mostly private, although there wasn't a door, only a wall that separated it from the bedroom. The toilet was in its own little closet, so at least there was that. The exterior walls of the space were made of white opaque glass, which was a relief. She wasn't sure she was ready to test the theory as to whether someone could see in or not.

"There's a chance I didn't hide it as well as I thought," Brady said, releasing her hand and walking over to the shower to turn on the water.

"Hide what?"

"My interest in you."

He said it as though it wasn't new.

Reilly cocked her head. "How long have you been interested in me, Mr. McCord?"

His smirk was slow and wicked.

Her gaze shifted to his chest when he began pulling his shirt off. Oh, man. The man's body could've been cast in stone and placed with Greek god statues. He was impressively built. So much so her mouth watered just looking at him.

"A while," he said, and it took a moment for her to realize what he meant.

"You've been interested in me for a while?"

He nodded.

"But you never said anything?"

"What was I supposed to say?"

"Oh, I don't know." She moved closer. "How about, hey, Reilly, would you like to go out sometime?"

Color rose in his cheeks. Was he blushing?

"Did it have something to do with the age difference?"

Brady unbuttoned his jeans but then walked over to her. As she waited for him to respond, he pulled her shirt over her head. When it was off, she turned away from him, allowing him to unhook her bra. When she turned back, she let the bra fall to the floor, keeping her arms down, enjoying the way he admired her breasts.

"Fuck," he whispered, stepping forward and cupping both with his big hands.

She immediately remembered the way he'd fucked her tits last night. No one had ever done that before, and she found it ridiculously hot. And the way he'd pinched her nipples ... who knew pain could morph into pleasure that way?

He kneaded her breasts for a moment before releasing her. She instantly missed the warmth.

"Take off your pants," Brady commanded. "I need to touch you some more."

While he undressed, Reilly did the same. She managed not to ogle him too much, but she couldn't say the same for him. He was staring, which allowed her to walk into the shower first. The water was hot, but not too hot, so she stepped under the spray, tipped her head back, and got her hair wet. Her eyes were closed when she felt Brady's hands on her tits again. This time, he plucked her nipples, making her gasp.

"I need to suck them," he said, but she wasn't sure if he was telling her or simply relaying a fact.

She tipped her head up and watched as he leaned down and took one into his mouth. He sucked on her nipple, gently at first, then more firmly. He released her, scraping his teeth on the sensitive tip as he did. He then did the same with her other breast.

When he stood up, his eyes were hooded, and his lips were darker from teasing her.

"You are so fucking beautiful," he rasped, sliding his hand behind her neck and bringing her forward until their lips melded together.

Reilly got lost in the kiss, sliding her hands over his smooth, warm skin, reacquainting herself with all the dense muscle, the perfectly sculpted planes and angles of his torso, and the finely rounded globes of his ass.

"It's been years," Brady said against her lips.

Reilly pulled back, not sure what he was talking about.

He met her gaze and brushed her hair back from her face. "I've wanted you for years, Reilly."

"You could've had me," she admitted.

"I wanted you to be ready for me."

She didn't know what that meant. "Ready for you how?"

His eyes locked with hers. "Now that I've got you, I never want to let you go."

Smiling, she leaned into him, wrapping her arms around his waist. "I know the feelin'."

"I'm serious." His expression matched his words. "I want you here with me, Reilly."

Assuming he meant tonight, she leaned in and kissed him again. "I'm not goin' anywhere. Promise."

BRADY REALIZED REILLY DIDN'T UNDERSTAND WHAT HE meant. He was being literal. He wanted her there with him every night. Forever.

Yeah, he was moving fast, but he didn't care. He'd wanted her for so long, it felt like the natural progression at this point. He wasn't getting any younger, and he was ready to settle down. This time forever. He didn't worry that he was caught up in a whirlwind the way he had been with Alyssa because he knew Reilly. He knew everything about her, and he loved every single thing.

However, he decided to table the discussion until later. For now, he was content to have her with him.

Sliding his hand between her legs, he teased her cleft. "You're wet."

She giggled. "I'm in the shower."

That made him smile. "Are you tellin' me I'm not doin' my job correctly?"

"I never said that." She giggled again when he backed her up against the wall.

He slipped a finger into her tight, wet pussy, watching her face as he did. Her eyes closed, and a soft moan escaped as she rocked against his hand.

"More," she whimpered, spreading her legs wider.

Brady added another finger.

"Oh, yes."

She was so damn beautiful. He loved watching her as pleasure coursed through her. It was an incredible sight.

It was all he could do not to drive himself inside her. He wanted to. God, he wanted to. But he wanted to slow this down. For a little while, at least. He wanted to show her it wasn't only sex for him. Although he wasn't sure she would have a problem with it if it were.

"Make me come," she begged, rocking faster. "Fuck me, Brady."

He gave her what she asked for, making her come with his fingers, then kissed her while she came down from her orgasm. When she reached for his cock, he sidestepped.

"Not yet. I'm gonna feed you first. Then we can play some more."

"Tease."

They made out for several more minutes, with him practically holding her down to keep her from reaching for him. Brady knew he would've caved, given half a chance.

"You finish showering. I'll start cookin'. I'll leave a robe out for when you're done."

Resisting her was the hardest thing he'd ever done, but he extricated himself from her arms and got out. He dried off, pulled on his robe, and then grabbed another from the closet for her. He kept from watching her as she soaped her body, knowing if he did, he would be right back in there with her.

Twenty minutes later, she joined him downstairs. She was wearing his robe, which covered her like a blanket, reaching to her dainty ankles. It was the sexiest thing he'd ever seen in his life.

"Mmm. Smells good."

"BLT-As," he told her.

Reilly's eyes widened. "Really?"

He knew they were her favorite. Plus, it was simple—one egg over hard, with bacon, lettuce, tomato, and avocado on toast.

"Have a seat," he said, gesturing toward the barstool with the spatula.

Once she was seated, he made her sandwich, then passed it over before returning to make his own.

"I have a question to ask you," she said while chewing her first bite.

He cocked an eyebrow, urging her to ask.

She finished chewing. "Would you go to my parents' tomorrow night for dinner? With me, I mean. As *my* plus one."

Brady flipped the egg in the pan but didn't look at her.

"Unless you've got other plans," she quickly added. "I'm sorry. I didn't think to ask."

"I don't," he admitted.

"Are you worried what they'll say? About you and me, I mean?"

He looked up then because he wanted her to know that didn't bother him at all. It was the opposite. What he wanted to do was to go over to her parents' house now and ask her father for permission to marry her. However, he didn't want to scare her off by admitting that.

"I want them to know," he said, hoping to reassure her.

Her relieved sigh was loud in the otherwise silent room.

"Is it because you miss your mom?"

Brady hadn't expected Reilly to go that route, but she'd hit the mark perfectly. For the most part, he could make it through the day without his chest squeezing too much. He missed his mother. They'd been close, and it had only been a year since she died. Last Christmas, he'd managed to make it through the holiday because he'd still been in a fog. This year, her absence was noticeable.

More so now that Reilly was here. He wanted nothing more than to call his mom and tell her he'd finally met the woman he could see himself with forever. She'd understood when he divorced Alyssa, and she always told him when he found the one, he would not have any doubts.

I have no doubts, Mom. None at all.

"What did you two do on Christmas?" Reilly asked, clearly taking his silence as confirmation.

He turned his attention back to the stove and finished making his sandwich.

"We would make popcorn and watch movies on Christmas Eve. I'd buy cookies and popcorn and come over that evening so we could hang out. I always spent the night. Then we went to your parents' house for dinner the next day." He grinned wide. "She hated cookin'. Like seriously hated it. But she didn't mind helpin' your mom."

Reilly laughed. "That sounds like fun," she said, her gaze lingering on him as she ate. "You've got great memories."

"I do, yes." Brady carried his plate to the bar. "And yes, Reilly, I'd be happy to go to your parents with you."

"Really?" Her eyes crinkled at the corners as though that was the best news she'd heard in a long time.

"Yeah. And I'd like to make some new memories this year. With you."

Reilly stopped chewing, and her eyes teared up. "I'd like that," she said around a mouthful of food.

She really was fucking adorable.

Seventeen

"You think it's safe to close?" Donovan asked Tate.

After their encounter in the storage room, Donovan dressed and returned to the front to unlock the door. That was four hours ago. Since then, they'd had two customers. One had purchased the last set of twinkling lights, the other a box of wine. Besides the woman who'd come in for toilet paper, no one in Coyote Ridge seemed to need anything that couldn't wait until Tuesday.

"I hope so," Tate said from his perch on the counter. "Otherwise, one of us is gonna have to go get food. I'm starvin'."

Donovan was, too. He hadn't bothered to eat when he'd gone with Brady to talk, and the granola bar he pilfered earlier had burned off long ago.

"You good with the diner?" Donovan offered as he headed for the front door to lock up.

When Tate didn't answer, he looked back to see he was staring at him with a blank expression.

"You do eat real food, right?"

Tate nodded. "Of course."

"So unless you're embarrassed to be seen with me…"

Tate shook his head. "No. Definitely not."

"So what's the hold-up?"

"I guess I just…"

Donovan went to the register to retrieve the cash and lock it in the safe, gesturing for Tate to continue.

"I didn't expect us to actually … go out."

Donovan frowned. "What kind of guys do you date?"

"What do you mean?"

"Surely they've taken you to dinner before."

Tate shrugged. "Once in a while."

That was certainly interesting.

"Well, then, this might be new for you. I like to eat, and I'm not big on cookin' for one, so I tend to go out. I don't usually eat alone, but I will if I'm hungry enough." He closed the register and took a slip of the receipt paper. "And at the moment, I am. But I'd much prefer you to go with me."

Donovan paused in front of Tate, who was still staring at him blankly.

"For the record, I'll also take you to the movies and clubs. Concerts. Once in a while, I'll have a work function. You opposed to any of that?"

Tate shook his head, but his lack of response concerned Donovan a bit. He decided to table that conversation until they were sitting at one. He really was starving.

"Good answer." Donovan grinned. "Now come on. Let's eat so I can take you back to my house and fuck you again. I fully intend to make up for missin' out this mornin'."

Tate's loud swallow made him laugh.

Twenty minutes later, they were sitting in a booth in the diner across from one another. The place was busier than he expected, but it didn't surprise him. It was Christmas Eve, and most of those people would likely be cooking tomorrow, so they were treating themselves to a timeout from kitchen duty tonight.

"Do you like to cook?" Donovan asked as they perused the menus while they waited for the waitress.

"On occasion." His eyes lifted. "That's not to say I'm good at it."

Donovan gave Tate a few minutes to settle. He still seemed somewhat uncomfortable, which was the opposite of how he usually was. When Tate was around Reilly, he never shut up. Without her here, he seemed to be at a loss for words.

The waitress did a drive-by, quickly jotting down what they wanted and delivering water and a basket of bread. Donovan ignored both, opting to keep his full attention on Tate.

"Okay, *sweetie*," he drawled, "what's on your mind?"

Tate's gaze snapped up. He huffed a laugh. "You're makin' fun of me."

"No. Of course not." He leaned back and tapped Tate's foot with his. "Relax. I won't ravish you in public."

Tate's smile remained.

Donovan leaned forward. "Unless you ask nicely."

"Careful," Tate said. "I might just do that."

"Careful," Donovan mocked. "I will follow through."

Tate gasped and continued to wipe the condensation off of his water glass.

"Did you ever get your schedule changed?"

Tate frowned. "What?"

"I heard you tellin' Reilly that you were tryin' to change shifts."

"Oh." His eyebrows remained angled downward. "You were listening?"

"I've listened to nearly everything you've said for the past two years."

"Really?"

"Why so surprised?"

Tate shrugged.

"Did you? Get it changed?"

"Yeah," Tate answered. "Finally. I'm workin' twenty-four-hour shifts on Tuesdays, and I alternate between twelve and twenty-four every other week on Thursdays and Fridays."

"So you're free on weekends? For the most part, right?"

"I usually sleep most of Saturday, but yeah."

Donovan continued to watch him. He could've watched the man all day. He was fascinated by Tate; there was no denying that.

"Am I movin' too fast for you?" he asked, trying to figure out why Tate was so quiet.

"No."

"Then you mind tellin' me what's wrong?"

"Nothing." Tate's eyebrows rose when Donovan continued to stare. "Seriously."

"Not buyin' it."

"Fine." Tate exhaled roughly. "I'm surprised you wanted to go out with me."

"Because you're so good in bed, that's the only place I should keep you?"

Tate barked a laugh, clearly taken aback by the question. "Of course not."

"You've known me for a long time, Tate. I'm a pretty sociable guy, right?"

"Yeah."

"I don't spend a lot of time at home. But if it bothers you that I want to take you out, just—"

"It doesn't." Tate smiled, and this time, it was shy. "This is nice. I just wasn't expecting it."

"Which is why you ran away this mornin'. We're past that, Tate." Donovan leaned forward again, this time reaching for Tate's hand. "I'm not in the closet, and I haven't been for a long damn time. You haven't been either."

Tate continued to watch him.

"So what do you say we enjoy this?"

"Okay."

Donovan nodded and released Tate's hand before grabbing his water glass.

"Oh, and you should know. Tomorrow, when we go to my parents' house for dinner, you'll be *my* date. Not Reilly's."

This time, the smile on Tate's face was radiant, and Donovan felt the man relax.

TATE WASN'T SURE WHY HE'D BEEN SO surprised when Donovan asked him to dinner, but it had struck him as odd. For whatever reason, he hadn't been able to shake it. Not at first. He should've known Donovan would realize something was wrong.

But the truth was, there wasn't. Everything was exactly right, and maybe that was what had him all freaked out.

Tate had spent much of his adult life with a serious crush on this man. Even in his wildest dreams, he never thought he might be in this situation one day. Sitting across from him, sharing a meal and casual conversation. He'd fantasized about Donovan so many times, but mostly when he was jacking off because that seemed to be the only place it was appropriate.

But this … this was real. This was the two of them enjoying one another's company. And while it started awkwardly, the conversation had taken a nice turn. Donovan knew far more about Tate than he thought, but it didn't seem enough for him. He asked questions, and Tate answered them as best he could. Nothing too intrusive, and eventually, he began to relax.

"Can I get you some dessert?" the waitress asked as she stepped up to the table and refilled Tate's water glass.

Donovan looked at him.

He looked at Donovan.

"Do you need a minute to think about it?"

Donovan decided for them, looking up at the waitress. "I think we'll skip dessert. We've got somewhere to be."

They did? That was certainly news to Tate.

"Lemme grab your check. I'll—"

"Put it on this." Donovan handed her his credit card before she walked away.

She nodded, tucking the card in her pocket before pausing at the next table to ask the same questions.

"Did you need to be somewhere?" Tate asked when she was out of earshot.

"No."

"So, where do you need to be?"

"*We*," Donovan clarified. "*We* need to be somewhere."

Okay. That didn't tell Tate anything at all aside from he was being invited to tag along.

"Relax." Donovan tapped his foot.

Tate wasn't sure why he liked that Donovan did that. Every so often, he would feel Donovan's boot bump his shoe, and it was a subtle reminder that they were together. He tried to recall whether anyone else he'd dated had done something similar. He didn't think so.

Donovan pulled out his phone and looked at it. His forehead creased when he started typing. It seemed to go on forever before, finally, the wrinkle smoothed out, and a smirk formed on his lips.

God, the man had incredibly nice lips.

When Donovan's eyes lifted, Tate looked away quickly, not wanting him to know he was staring.

"You're damn cute, you know that?" Donovan smiled before taking the receipt and the credit card from the waitress when she returned to the table.

Within seconds, Donovan scribbled his name on the receipt, tucked his credit card back in his wallet, and got out of the booth. Tate followed his lead, getting to his feet and letting Donovan lead him out of the restaurant with a hand on his shoulder. It was such a possessive gesture, and for some reason, Tate's dick thought it was the sexiest thing ever. He had to adjust himself as they walked to Donovan's truck. He tried to do so discreetly, but he should've known Donovan would notice.

Donovan opened his door for him, but he didn't let him get in.

Tate gasped when Donovan tipped his head back, gripping his chin firmly, and leaned in until they were nearly nose to nose.

"I want to take you home, strip you down, and do dirty fuckin' things to you."

Tate's mental hand shot high in the air and waved. *Yes. God, yes!*

"But first, I want to show you somethin'. No questions."

He nodded, still too shocked to speak. But he wasn't too stunned to kiss Donovan back when his mouth descended. It was chaste and sweet, and it only amped up his adrenaline and made his cock throb.

Donovan was chuckling when he pulled back. "Get in."

Tate got in.

Eighteen

"Mr. McCord?" Reilly called out as she walked down the stairs to join Brady on the couch.

After lunch, they'd gone upstairs to his bedroom and taken a nap. She hadn't realized how tired she was until she lay down. She'd gone up there hoping to rekindle what they'd started in the shower. But that turned into a four-hour nap, which wouldn't bode well for her sleeping tonight, but it was Christmas Eve, so she figured that was okay.

When she woke up, she was alone, but she found Brady in his office, sitting at his drafting table. Working. Apparently, that was what he did in his spare time. After that, he'd given her a full tour of the house, showing off the impressive back patio with the stone fireplace and outdoor furniture nicer than the stuff she had in her house.

The tour had ended in an afternoon walk, which, to her dismay, had required her to put on clothes. They'd returned a few minutes ago, so she'd excused herself to go upstairs to change back into his robe. She was becoming quite fond of it, actually.

She took the steps down slowly, trying to scrounge up the nerve to follow through with her seduction plan. It was so much easier to think about doing it than to actually *do it*.

"I have to tell you somethin'," she told Brady now, licking her lips and swallowing the lump of nerves that made her voice husky.

"You can tell me anything." His gaze shifted from the television to her as she strolled toward him.

Her pussy clenched with anticipation, but she forged ahead.

"I've been a bad girl," she told him.

She could tell he was attempting to hide a smile, his expression remaining somewhat impassive despite the slight curl of his lip and the crinkle at the corners of his eyes. "Have you now?"

She chewed on her bottom lip and nodded. "Very bad."

His throat worked on a swallow, and his eyes narrowed as he watched her. "What did you do that's so bad?"

"I stole your car."

"I recall that," he said, sitting up as she approached.

Reilly stopped directly in front of him. "I think I need to be punished."

He leaned forward, sliding his hand under the robe and cupping the back of her leg, urging her closer. His touch alone set her on fire.

His dark eyes lifted to her face. "What do you think your punishment should be?"

Spank me, Mr. McCord. Spank me, please.

Again, it was easier to think about than to say, so she went with, "Whatever you think is fair."

"Why do you think I should be fair, sweet baby?"

Reilly swallowed as her clit pulsed from the heat she saw in his eyes. She liked the direction he was going. It seemed to be running right alongside where her dirty thoughts were headed.

She shrugged, feeling her cheeks warm.

"Well, I think we'll start by removin' this," Brady said, tugging at the tie on her robe.

She stepped closer when he loosened it, allowing him to open it. Cool air wafted over her overheated skin, although it was warm in the house.

"Take it off," he instructed. "All the way."

Reilly let it fall from her shoulders, down her arms, then pool on the floor at her feet.

Brady sat back and looked at her, not hiding his approval. Even if he had, she would've known he liked what he saw because she could see the outline of his cock beneath the robe he still wore.

"Maybe I could take care of you," she suggested. "You know, as punishment."

"Take care of me?"

She nodded, then bit her lower lip before saying, "Sucking your cock."

His lips parted, and she knew she had surprised him. It made her feel bolder.

"You want to suck my cock?"

"Yes." She met his stare and added, "Yes, *Mr. McCord*."

"Aw, Jesus." He patted his thighs. "Come here. I think we'll deal with your punishment first."

Not sure what he wanted her to do, Reilly allowed Brady to guide her. He positioned her so that she was draped across his lap.

She giggled. As hot as it was, she still found it oddly amusing. Silly, almost. At least until his big hand caressed the backs of her thighs, then higher, lightly teasing her flesh. Arousal drowned everything else out, heating her from the inside. His hand felt good. Slightly callused, abrading her skin in the most sensual way.

Although she knew she was supposed to remain in character, it was difficult. She giggled, imagining what she looked like. Or Brady, for that matter.

The giggle died a sweet death when he rubbed along the seam of her pussy, teasing her folds. She gasped.

His hand returned to her ass. "Have you ever been spanked before?"

"No." It was the truth. Not as a child or as an adult. She was always open for kinkier bedroom games, but the men she was with rarely ventured into taboo territory.

"Have you ever spanked anyone before?" she asked.

"No."

She believed him.

"But I'm lookin' forward to doin' it for the first time."

"Me, too," she whispered when his finger glided between her ass cheeks. When he teased her hole, she whimpered.

"Have you ever been *fucked* here?"

"No."

"Have you ever been *fingered* here?"

"No."

"Have you ever been *licked* here?"

A shiver racked her body. "No."

"But you want to."

It wasn't a question, but she nodded anyway. She loved sex. To the point, she got herself off with her vibrator at least once a day. She definitely preferred when it wasn't a solo endeavor, but she'd always been hesitant, wanting to get to know someone before she jumped into bed with them. She didn't have that problem with Brady. She'd known him all her life. She trusted him.

He leaned over and bit her butt cheek, making her squirm and giggle. As soon as she tried to move, he placed one hand across her back and the other—

Reilly cried out when he spanked her. It was harder than she anticipated, but the fire that licked at her skin made her pussy clench and release. She choked off the giggle and moaned, hoping he would do it again.

He gave her a moment to recover, caressing her ass. The instant his hand lifted, she tried to brace for it. He held off just long enough for her to exhale before he landed the second blow.

She squirmed, then moaned when he slid his finger into her pussy.

"Oh, fuck, Reilly. You're drenched."

She most definitely was. The whole role-playing thing was certainly an aphrodisiac. And the actual spanking. That was hot, too.

"Three more," Brady warned, then spanked her again, this time on her other cheek.

Reilly rocked her hips, attempting to get friction on her clit. Brady shifted his leg, making it impossible, and then he spanked her again. This time, he landed both swats in rapid succession.

"Okay?" he asked, running his hands over her back.

"More than," she said, grinning, although her butt stung a little.

"Are you cold?"

She shook her head.

"Good. Because I want you to stay just like that."

Before she could ask what he had in mind, Brady shifted. She wasn't sure what he was doing, but a moment later, she heard a click, and it sounded like a lid being closed on a bottle. The next thing she knew, something firm pressed against her asshole. It glided easily between her cheeks, but when she tried to twist to see what it was, Brady pressed his hand on her back.

"Relax."

She took a deep breath and exhaled slowly.

"Do you trust me?"

"Yes."

"You didn't even hesitate," he noted.

"I didn't have to. I trust you, Brady."

That must've been the permission he was looking for because he pressed something against her asshole. He teased her with it, rimming her hole before gently pushing it in.

"It's a vibrator," he finally said. "A very slim one."

"You had a vibrator just lyin' around?" She wasn't sure how she felt about that.

He chuckled. "You sell them at the store."

Reilly skimmed her memories, trying to remember when she'd ordered—"Oh, yeah."

She chuckled softly. They were called personal massagers, but she remembered getting them. Tate had dared her to. When they came in, he tried to convince her to send them back, but she told him she wanted to see the reactions when people saw them. To this day, she'd never sold any.

But obviously, someone had since Brady had one.

"Does it hurt?"

"Uh-uh," she said, relaxing as he continued to tease her.

"One day, I'm gonna fuck you here," he said, his voice gruff.

Before she should tell him that one day should be today, he turned the vibrator on, and she squealed.

Brady chuckled. "Relax. Enjoy."

His other hand, the one resting on her back, moved. A moment later, the television came on. She stared at it and then laughed when he hit play on *The Grinch* movie. The one with Jim Carrey as the Grinch.

"That's better," he said, his hand returning to her back, the other continuing to torment her with the vibrator.

Time ceased to exist as she endured the sensual torment while pretending to pay attention to the movie.

BRADY WASN'T SURE HOW HE SURVIVED THE past couple of hours. It was a form of sexual torture, no doubt about it. He'd spent that time teasing every inch of Reilly's perfect body while she pretended to relax. She'd started across his lap, then *in* his lap, and ended with her head resting on his thigh while he massaged her beautiful tits.

When the movie finally ended, he knew he wasn't going to last much longer. As it was, he hadn't paid a damn bit of attention, looking mostly at his hands as he fondled and stroked the woman in his lap.

"Mr. McCord," Reilly said in that seductive rasp he loved so much.

"Hmm?"

"Do you think perhaps you could fuck me now?"

Oh, hell. He wasn't sure what he'd done to deserve her. She was completely out of his league in every way, but he was head over heels for her.

"I think now would be good," he said, his voice gravel rough.

He helped her sit up, then tugged her arm, urging her back into his lap. This time, he had her straddling his thighs so he could taste her sweet lips. When he kissed her, she jerked on the tie of his robe, then shoved at the cotton to get it off his arms. She was already naked, and it didn't take him but a second to catch up.

The next thing Brady knew, Reilly had him in her hand, caressing him so sweetly before she lifted her hips and guided him right where he wanted to be.

She gently eased down on him, her hands moving to his shoulders as she tipped her head back and moaned softly. He watched her, admiring the generous swell of her breasts and the sleek column of her neck. He had to grit his teeth because the pleasure was so intense. Unlike anything he'd felt in a damn long time. She was so hot and so fucking wet he slid into her easily. Too easily.

He wasn't sure anything had ever felt this fucking good. The way her inner walls stroked him as he sank in to the hilt. She lifted, lowered, and he gasped for breath, trying to figure out what was missing. Something was—

"Fuck," he grunted, holding her hips still.

"What's wrong?"

"Condom," he said, ashamed that he'd been too blinded by lust to think about precautions.

Reilly remained where she was, his cock fully seated inside her. She cupped his face, her fingers soft and cool against his skin.

"I'm on the pill," she said softly. "And I haven't been with anyone in a really long time."

He understood what she was saying, but he still felt like an ass for not taking the appropriate measures beforehand.

"Brady," she whispered, pressing her lips to the corner of his mouth. "If you want a condom, I'll get one."

He opened his eyes and got lost in her light-green gaze. She was so fucking beautiful.

"I trust you," she said, kissing the other corner of his mouth. "Do you trust me?"

"Always."

She kept her eyes locked with his as she began to move, lifting her hips, sliding off his cock until he was almost entirely out of her. Then she lowered again, her pussy walls caressing every inch of him.

Part of him couldn't believe this was happening. It felt surreal. Overwhelmingly so.

"Reilly," he whispered, wrapping his arms around her and pulling her against him as he kissed her.

She whimpered, rocking her hips, continuing to ignite sparks where their bodies were joined.

"God, baby, you feel so good," he rasped, pressing his forehead to hers, afraid to let her see the emotion that was no doubt glittering in his eyes. He couldn't help it. This was different. And it wasn't solely about how fucking good it felt. She trusted him.

Brady slipped his hand between their bodies, finding her clit with this thumb. He applied gentle pressure, which increased each time she rocked forward.

"Yes," she hissed.

He pulled back and looked into her eyes. "Can you come like this?"

She nodded.

"Not yet," he told her when her pussy fluttered around his cock. "Not yet, sweet baby."

Brady satisfied himself with watching as she rode him, taking them both high with every passing second. Reilly wasn't in a hurry, and neither was he. He let the sensations linger, each one more intense than the last as she fucked him.

When she cupped her breasts and lifted them toward his mouth, he leaned in and sucked on her nipples, alternating between them as she continued the perfect rolling motion that caused a tingling in his spine.

She whimpered when he curled his arm around her and held her in place, impaled on his cock. He rolled her beneath him on the couch, shifting over her so they were touching from chest to knee. He began pumping into her, brushing her hair back from her face as she stared up at him. Her green eyes glittered as she watched him watching her.

"It's perfect," she whispered.

He maintained a leisurely pace. "What is?"

"All of it. You. Me." She curled her arms under his, holding onto him. "*This.*"

Brady tilted his pelvis so that he added friction against her clit as he fucked her with slow, deep strokes.

"Yes…" Reilly spread her knees wider, allowing more friction where she wanted it. "Just like that… oh, Brady."

"You undo me, sweet baby," he whispered.

Reilly smiled. "Ditto."

When he drove into her harder, Reilly shifted, allowing him to go deeper.

When he began pounding into her, she grabbed his arms, holding herself still to maximize the pleasure for both of them.

"Come for me, Reilly," he said softly, still holding her gaze.

Another smile pulled at her sweet lips, and a second later, her head tilted back, her body clasping him as she whimpered and moaned.

She buried her face in his neck and held on while he made love to her in the sweetest way he'd ever experienced. He gauged how close she was by her soft whimpers and moans.

"Brady…"

Her pussy clenched tightly, fluttering around his cock.

"Oh, God," she cried out, her arms tightening around him as her body tensed beneath his.

Brady ground his teeth together, holding on for one … more … minute.

Reilly brought her lips to his ear and whispered, "I love you."

He wasn't sure she meant for him to hear it, but those three words sent him soaring.

"Come for me," he demanded gruffly. "Come for me so I can come inside you."

Reilly cried out his name, her nails digging into his flesh as she shattered underneath him. He let go, soaring into an ethereal existence, floating on pleasure so intense he wanted to cry.

Nineteen

Donovan was surprised Tate didn't ask questions when he drove to his parents' house.

He still didn't ask questions after Donovan ran in and grabbed the thermos of hot chocolate and the baggie full of marshmallows that his mother had prepared at his request. She'd had a knowing smile when he told her he couldn't stay, then she passed him two disposable coffee cups and told him good luck.

It wasn't until Donovan was steering the truck into the small alcove at the lake's edge that Tate finally said, "What are we doin' here?"

"Come on," he told him, grabbing the thermos, the marshmallows, and the two paper cups.

If he'd planned this, he would've brought a blanket with him, but it was a spur-of-the-moment thing, and it was a wonder he'd thought to get the hot chocolate, so they would have to settle for sitting on the tailgate. He pressed the button on the key fob to lower the tailgate and waited for Tate to join him.

"What is this place?" Tate asked as he hopped up onto the tailgate.

"Where I like to come to think things through."

"Do you come here a lot?"

Donovan passed him one of the paper cups and then opened the thermos. "I used to. Not so much anymore."

"Because you don't need to think things through?"

He chuckled as he poured the hot chocolate into Tate's cup. "I still think things through, but there's little time to slow down. I want to. I *need* to, but I rarely do."

"Marshmallows?" Donovan held the baggy up for him.

Tate took the bag. "Thanks."

"The only people who know I come here are my mom and Reilly," Donovan explained as he poured more chocolate into his cup.

"Why'd you bring me?" Tate asked, sipping from his cup as the steam rose.

"Because I wanted to make our first date memorable."

He saw Tate flinch with surprise. "First date?"

"The diner's nice and all," he teased, "but you deserve better."

"I like the diner, sweetie," Tate said, then grunted. "Sorry. Habit."

Donovan chuckled as he stared out at the water that glittered in the moonlight. "The first time I came out here was the night you came to live with my parents and Reilly."

He could feel Tate's eyes on him.

"After our conversation, I was so angry," Donovan continued because he wanted to share this story with Tate. "I was livid that your mother did what she did. That she even had the ability to dampen the fire inside you."

"She didn't," Tate countered.

"She did," Donovan argued. "On a certain level. You're still you, yes. Your fire still burns bright and hot, but she tried to put it out, and I was furious with her for that. I came here that night, trying to figure out exactly what I was going to say to her when I went to her house."

Tate gasped softly.

Donovan glanced at him. "I didn't go. I wanted to. My mother found me here and talked me out of it." He looked back at the water and gripped his cup with both hands. "Told me there are people in this world who see others as broken. They're the ones who are truly broken, and words'll never fix them. She told me that the only thing we can do is live our lives to the fullest, and those who've decided to become spectators would hopefully feel the loss when they're standin' on the sidelines.

"It took me a while to get past what she did," Donovan continued. "I've been out here a hundred times since then. Like I said, I come here to think." He cut his gaze to Tate again. "The last time I came here was back in January. I'd stopped by my parents' house to chat. You and Reilly were there. I saw y'all through the window. The four of you laughing about something. I didn't go in. I should have, but something stopped me from opening the front door. I came here instead."

Tate took a sip, and Donovan could tell he was listening.

"Reilly must've seen me because she followed me here. We sat just like this, staring out at the water while she pretended she wasn't freezin' her ass off." He chuckled at the memory. "She wanted to tell me somethin', and it took her a minute to get to the point. You know how she is."

Tate laughed. "Oh, I know. What did she need to tell you?"

Donovan sighed and smiled. "She told me she saw the way I was lookin' at you. That she was onto my game." He dropped his chin, but the grin remained. "It's never been a game, but I never intended to act on my attraction. It felt … wrong."

"Wrong?"

Donovan moved past that explanation, opting to continue with his story. "Reilly told me that night that you had a crush on me."

"She didn't!" Tate gasped. "Oh, God. Of course she did. That girl has a problem keepin' secrets."

Donovan laughed. "Yes, she does. Especially when she thinks it'll benefit someone else."

"What did you … uh … say to that?" Tate asked.

"I told her you had a boyfriend."

Tate nodded, then looked out at the water. "Ben. Right."

"She told me he was a creep." Donovan chuckled. "And she assured me I could take him."

Tate laughed. "She wanted you to beat up Ben? That's priceless."

"That secret intrigued me," Donovan admitted. "Enough that I might've been obsessing a bit."

"If it's any consolation, I didn't notice," Tate said softly. "I wish I had."

"I almost did somethin' about it last summer," he admitted, figuring he might as well get it all out there. "We were all at my folks' place, in the pool. I don't know why, but I wanted to kiss you, but it hadn't been long since you'd broken up with that guy. I used that as an excuse. Told myself you might go back to him."

"Don't blame you there. My history of takin' him back's not stellar."

Donovan cut his gaze to Tate.

"But we're definitely over now," Tate said adamantly.

He nodded, ensuring Tate he understood. "You have to be."

Tate's brow furrowed. "Why?"

"Because you're mine now," he said, holding his stare and ensuring Tate heard the sincerity in his tone. "It's been a long fuckin' time since I've wanted anyone the way I want you. Now that I have you—and I do have you, right?"

"Yes," Tate gasped softly.

"Now that I have you, I don't intend to let you go."

EVEN AS DONOVAN'S WORDS RANG IN HIS ears, Tate's chest swelled to the point he thought it might explode.

"I made a wish," he blurted, feeling his face flame as soon as the words were out of his mouth.

"A wish?" Donovan cocked an eyebrow. "For?"

"You," he admitted, keeping his eyes on the water. "To kiss me. Back when I was in high school. A senior. My senior year. That was what I wished for. We do that. Me and Reilly. We make wishes every year. Hot chocolate wishes, we call them. Started when we were in, I don't know, the third grade? It doesn't matter. We've done them every year. This year, we took the ones from 2018 and renewed them. Same wish. You. Me. Kiss."

Tate was rambling. He knew it, and he couldn't do a damn thing about it. His mouth wouldn't stop, and his brain wasn't issuing the shut-up directive fast enough.

"I didn't think it would happen. Ever. Certainly not ... you know ... what we ended up doin' last night. I mean, I've had a crush on you for a long time, but that's all it was. A crush. Unrequited and all that. But I—"

Donovan reached over, his fingertips on his chin, urging Tate to face him. As soon as he did, Donovan cupped his face and kissed him.

Tate sighed into it, relishing the gentle press of Donovan's mouth to his. He leaned forward, keeping their lips together, when Donovan got down from the tailgate and moved to stand in front of him. Tate was aware of his hot chocolate being removed from his hand, freeing him to slide his arms into Donovan's coat when he stepped between Tate's legs.

"Full transparency," Donovan said against his mouth, pulling back just enough to meet Tate's gaze. "I had my mom spike the hot chocolate."

"I know." He grinned, staring up at the man who'd changed his world in ways Tate had never expected. "For the record, Reilly, God love her, can't get the recipe right no matter how hard she tries."

Donovan chuckled, then slid his hand across Tate's cheek, his expression sobering. "I want to take you home, Tate. I want to keep you there. Can I take you home?"

"Yes."

"Will you stay?"

Tate wasn't sure whether he was referring to one night or the rest of his life. Either way, the answer was the same. "Yes."

"Good." Donovan stepped back, causing Tate's hands to fall from under his coat. "Now come on. Let's warm you up."

"I'm not cold," Tate said as he slid down from the tailgate.

"Tell that to your fuckin' hands," Donovan grumbled.

On the short drive to Donovan's house, Tate stared out the window, grinning to himself. When they passed Brady's house, he noticed Reilly's truck was parked out front. He almost mentioned it to Donovan, then swallowed the words before they could escape. The last thing he wanted was to bring Reilly into this. He would certainly be texting her later, but for now, he figured they could both enjoy spending Christmas Eve with the men they'd been pining for for so long.

Tate had been to Donovan's house numerous times over the years. Birthdays, holidays, Sunday night football. However, he'd never been here without Reilly, and he realized it felt different.

Not worse, not better. Just different.

They walked in through the garage. When they were in the kitchen, Donovan emptied his pockets, tossing his wallet, keys, and phone on the counter before shrugging out of his coat. As soon as he did, he grabbed Tate's hand and dragged him through the living room and down the hallway to his bedroom.

Tate didn't have time to wonder what was going to happen now that they were here. He was grateful for that because he'd been nervous enough for most of the night. He figured if he kept it up, he might give Donovan a complex.

As soon as they were in the room, Donovan released him to flip on the wall sconces, which provided enough ambient light to see the enormous king-sized bed, plush black comforter, and variety of patterned throw pillows on top.

Tate was taking it all in when Donovan stepped in front of him, filling his view with his big muscular body. Tate tipped his head back. Donovan was watching him, his green eyes churning with heat.

They came together in a spark of passion that blazed through him as Donovan stripped them both, moving closer and closer to the bed while leaving a trail of clothes behind them on the floor. All Tate could do was hold on as Donovan wrapped one big arm around him, kissing him roughly while he jerked the bedding off the bed, sending it toppling to the floor.

Then they were horizontal, Donovan pinning him to the bed with his weight. Tate didn't let him go, wanting him to stay just like that so he could feel the heat of his body and the steady rise and fall of his chest as he panted while kissing him with devastating urgency.

"Last night was about foreplay," Donovan whispered. "Right now, I just need to be inside you."

Tate nodded because he needed the same thing. It was all he could do not to writhe and plead when Donovan sat on his haunches, producing a condom out of thin air and rolling it on. He was eternally grateful that the man had the ability to think about lube because Tate was so worked up he couldn't remember his own freaking name, and as eager as he was, dry was going to hurt.

"Keep your eyes open," Donovan said when he loomed above him once more. "Put your legs around me."

Tate did, pulling his knees back and cradling his hips while the head of Donovan's cock probed his hole.

Donovan grunted, his lips twisting as he slowly pushed inside him, stretching him to the point of pain. Tate breathed through it because it was nothing compared to the complete euphoria that consumed him as they became one.

Despite the urgency that fizzed in the air, Donovan took his time, fucking him deep and slow, sending shards of ecstasy bursting through his bloodstream as he succumbed to the intensity. When his eyes closed of their own volition, Donovan barked for him to open them. And when he whimpered Donovan's name, a smirk would form as he watched him.

It was better than anything Tate had ever felt, and he knew without a doubt that he was forever ruined.

"Let me love you, Tate," Donovan whispered, shifting so he could continue pumping his hips at a different angle, taking them both to the inevitable breaking point.

"Yes," he rasped, sliding his fingers into Donovan's silky hair. "Love me. Please."

Donovan's eyes flashed with fire as he began rolling his hips faster, grunting with every delicious thrust.

"I want you to come," Donovan groaned, propping himself on one arm so he could stroke Tate's cock.

Tate cried out, the pleasure too much to contain.

"Come for me, Tate. Let me watch you come apart."

The rough stroke of Donovan's hand and the gentle thrust of his cock had Tate's spine tingling, the electricity building until he was sure he was going to shatter into a million pieces.

"Oh, God!" Tate bucked his hips. "Oh, fuck."

"That's it, baby. Come for me."

Tate's muscles went rigid as his cock exploded, sending streams of cum onto his chest for the second time that day.

"Fuck, that's beautiful," Donovan growled as he began pounding into Tate harder, deeper, faster.

A second later, he came with Tate's name echoing off the walls.

When he fell to Tate's side, he was gasping for air, his arm draped across him, never mind the fact it would require them both to shower.

"If you even think about disappearing on me, I'll hunt you down, bare your ass, and paddle you until my handprint has a permanent residence on your skin."

Tate grinned, turning his head toward Donovan. "I'm not goin' anywhere."

"Good." Donovan moved closer. "Let's get cleaned up, then you should get some sleep. There's a rumor Santa comes during the night, and you might want to be ready."

Tate laughed.

Not too long after they showered, he fell asleep in Donovan's arms, with a smile permanently etched on his face.

Twenty

REILLY CAME AWAKE AS THE DAY WAS getting underway.

Considering the entire house was made of glass, she didn't have much choice. As she lay there, staring out the windows, listening to Brady breathe heavily beside her, she wondered how he managed. Sure, the house was great, but it felt like she was in a fishbowl. Or maybe a terrarium was a better word for it since, you know, a lack of water.

She grinned, stretching to see if she was still as sore as she'd been last night. After their encounter on the couch, Brady had brought her upstairs and made love to her. They'd fallen asleep after, then he'd woken her up and claimed her again.

There was a definite spontaneity to it when you didn't have to dig out a condom.

Reilly recalled how panicked Brady had been when they hadn't used one. It wasn't on purpose; she knew that. They'd simply been caught up in the moment. But it made her wonder why he'd been upset. Because he hadn't known she was on birth control?

"Mmm." Brady shifted, his arm sliding over her hips as he scooted closer. "Good mornin'."

"Merry Christmas," she said in response.

"It is that." He pressed a kiss to her shoulder.

"Do you want kids?" she blurted, then realized how off-subject that was for him. She'd been thinking about it, so it was only logical that she asked, but he'd been asleep.

Brady slowly lifted his head. "What?"

"Kids," she repeated, looking up at him. "Do you want them?"

To her surprise, he didn't seem panicked. She wondered why. Last night, she'd accidentally let it slip that she loved him. He hadn't said it back. It had niggled at her for a bit, but she pushed it out of her mind. This was new, and since she was the one who'd been in love with him for a long time, it was *really* new for him.

"I'm on birth control," she reminded him, wanting to ensure he knew it wasn't a risk at the moment. "It won't be an accident, I promise."

"Yes," he answered, his eyes skimming her face. "I want kids."

She nodded as though it made sense. She wasn't sure it did, though. Brady had been married to Alyssa for three years, and they'd never even tried to get pregnant. She knew because she'd heard Alyssa talking about it to his mother and hers. Back then, Alyssa came around as much as her brother and Brady did. They were practically a part of the family, so it was natural.

"Do *you* want kids?" Brady asked, propping his head on his hand and slowly pulling the sheet down, uncovering her breasts.

She glanced down as his fingers began to tease across her flesh, warming her from the inside out.

Reilly didn't hesitate. "Yes."

"With me?"

Her head snapped toward him. She wasn't sure how to answer that. Was it a trick? Was he trying to find out if she intended to trap him?

"Uhmmm…"

Brady smiled as he moved closer, urging her onto her side so she was facing away from him. He slid his arm under her head, his other hand pressing firmly on her pelvis, tipping her hips back. Realizing what he was doing, Reilly lifted her leg as his cock nudged her entrance from behind.

She sighed, relaxing against him as he filled her, spooning against her. They fit together so perfectly it was as though they'd been created for exactly this.

"I want to spend every day of my life wakin' up just like this," he whispered against her ear. "Holdin' you. Lovin' you."

There was the "L" word. It wasn't quite the same, but it caused a balloon of hope to swell in her chest.

"I want you in my bed every night," he continued as he rocked into her.

She wasn't sure what he was telling her or if this was merely *sex talk*. It didn't feel like it was, but she didn't want to jump to conclusions.

His arm tightened around her, his chin pressing against her shoulder as though he wanted to get closer than they were. She wasn't sure it was possible. She was surrounded by him, filled by him. She'd never felt anything as incredible as this moment.

"I love you, Reilly," he whispered, his words raspy and rough. "I want to spend the rest of my life with you. I want to marry you and make a family with you."

Amend that. *This* was the most incredible feeling in the world.

Reilly grabbed his arm, holding on tight.

"Tell me you want that, too."

"Yes, Brady. Yes. I want that, too."

He groaned, his hips punching forward as the urgency swept through the room, carrying them with it. He angled her hips, twisting her lower body until her knee was pressed to the mattress. It changed the angle, intensifying the pleasure. Brady drove in deep while she reached for his hip, holding herself against him, taking everything he was willing to give her.

She cried out when he slipped his hand under her, pressing his fingers on her clit, rubbing insistently. "Oh, oh, yes!"

Her orgasm blew through her with the force of a tidal wave. She shook violently as Brady drove into her several more times.

"Reilly ... oh, fuck ... Reilly."

He came, shuddering behind her, his arms holding her tightly.

A few minutes later, when the world righted and her lungs expanded again, Reilly felt more complete than she'd ever felt before.

Hot chocolate wishes had *nothing* on this.

DONOVAN WOKE TO HEAT BLASTING DOWN HIS left side and fingers teasing the hair on his chest.

"You could tease somethin' else if you'd like," he grumbled, letting Tate know he was awake.

The hand on his chest slid lower, over his ribs, his abs. "I could."

Before Tate could reach his prize, Donovan snatched his wrist, holding it firmly so his dick was out of the man's reach.

"That's not fair, sweetie. You said I'd only be punished if I *wasn't* in your bed this mornin'."

"No, I said I'd paddle your ass if you weren't. I didn't promise not to punish you for other things."

Tate chuckled when Donovan rolled toward him. "Like what?"

"Like makin' my dick so fuckin' hard," Donovan rasped against his neck. "And makin' me dream about doin' filthy things to you."

"You dreamed about me?"

Donovan didn't answer, simply began kissing his way down Tate's chest, then along the line that bisected his abs. He loved this body. How tight it was, how small it was. There were so many ways he wanted to defile this man.

Tate gasped when Donovan let the stubble on his chin lightly rub the head of his cock.

Another gasp sounded when he licked it.

"Let's see how limber you are," he said as he bent Tate's knee toward his chest and propped his shoulder under his thigh to keep him in that position.

Donovan was within sucking range of Tate's cock. And with him spread wide, he had plenty of access to the man's hole.

"This is what happens when you do what you're told and stay in bed," Donovan told him before leaning in and sucking Tate's cock between his lips.

He teased him for a second before lubing his finger with saliva and dragging it along Tate's taint to the puckered hole he'd obliterated last night.

"Ah," Tate sighed when Donovan pushed his finger slowly into his ass while he continued to suck and lick his cock.

"Hurt?"

"No."

Donovan wasn't sure he believed him, but he took his time, bringing Tate to the edge several times before giving him that final push that had him coming down Donovan's throat while his asshole spasmed around his finger.

As Tate drew air into his lungs, a happy grin on his face, Donovan moved over him. He found his mouth, kissing him slow and deep, letting him taste the lingering hint of cum on his tongue.

"Is that enough incentive to keep you where I want you?" he asked when he settled beside him, allowing Tate to drape his arm over his chest and his thigh over his leg.

"Yes."

Donovan trailed his fingers over Tate's back, along his spine, down to the crack of his ass.

"I want you to move in with me, Tate."

He felt the younger man's body tense.

"Too fast?" he asked, tipping his head toward Tate's.

"A little."

Donovan understood that. In fact, he'd expected Tate to say as much. The thing was, he didn't care how fast it was. He was ready to settle down and knew Tate was the man he wanted to spend the rest of his life with.

"No worries." He kissed Tate's forehead. "I'll ask you again tonight."

Tate laughed.

"If you say no, then I'll ask you tomorrow. And the next day. When you're ready, I'm ready, Tate. That won't change."

He didn't care if it took weeks or months to convince him this was where he wanted to be. Donovan was willing and eager.

Twenty-One

BRADY WAITED UNTIL REILLY WENT TO TAKE a shower before he grabbed his cell phone and carried it out onto the back porch. He figured he should probably be doing this face-to-face, but he didn't want to wait any longer.

He dialed Donovan's number, surprised when he answered on the first ring.

"Merry Christmas," he told his best friend.

"Same to you, man. What's up?"

"You got a minute?"

"Yeah. Tate's in the shower."

Brady swallowed past the lump in his throat and began pacing the length of the patio. "I wanted to ask you ... I mean, I plan to ask your dad later today, but I wanted to ask you first."

"You don't have to ask me," Donovan said, sounding like he had been expecting Brady to bring this up.

"I do have to ask," he countered.

"If you love my sister and she loves you, it doesn't matter what I say."

"But it does," Brady told him. "If, for some reason, you're against me bein' with her, I'd like to know."

Donovan sighed. "Brady, you are the absolute best man I know. For you to even think I might be against it..."

"I know," Brady said, understanding Donovan's disappointment. "It's just ... you're my best friend and my business partner. I don't want to do anything that'll change that."

"So you're sayin' you'd stop seein' Reilly if I had a problem with it?"

"No." Brady stopped walking. "I'm sayin' I want to do this the right way. I love her, and you're like a brother to me. I'm hopin'—"

Donovan laughed. "I'm fuckin' with you. And that was the right answer, by the way. She comes before all else."

"She does," Brady agreed. "I want to ask her to marry me. I know it might be too soon, but—"

"We both know time is nothing when you've found what you're lookin' for. You've got my blessing. And you know my dad'll say the same thing."

"I hope so." Brady sighed and resumed pacing. "How'd things go last night with Tate? I mean, you said he's in your shower, so I'm gonna assume that's a good thing."

"It is. I asked him to move in with me."

Wow. Holy shit. Brady honestly hadn't expected that. "And?"

"He turned me down." Donovan laughed. "That little shit's gonna keep me on my toes."

Brady grinned. "That's a good thing. You need someone who'll stand up to you."

"You're right. I do. Don't think for a second you've got it any easier with my sister. She's gonna give you a run for your money."

"And she'll enjoy it," Brady added, laughing because he knew it was true.

And he looked forward to every minute.

TATE HAD JUST FINISHED BRUSHING HIS TEETH when his gaze dropped to his cell phone for the fourth time in as many minutes.

Realizing he was going to get nothing done until he made the call, he dialed Reilly's number and prayed she would answer.

"What are you doing?" Reilly asked by way of greeting.

"I'm supposed to be in the shower," Tate whispered, hoping the sound of the water running would drown out the sound of him talking on the phone. "What are *you* doing?"

"Brady thinks I'm in the shower."

Tate laughed. Great minds and all that.

"I probably could've texted, but I wanted to hear your answer so I could tell if you're lyin'."

"My answer?" Reilly's curiosity echoed in her voice. "About what?"

"Donovan asked me to move in with him."

"What did you tell him?"

"Nothing."

Reilly laughed, but it was raspy and low. Clearly she was trying to be quiet, too.

"He asked if it was too fast. I told him a little."

"Is it?"

"No. But I didn't want *him* to know that. What if he's not really ready?"

Reilly giggled. "Seriously? You think D would've even brought it up if he wasn't?"

She had a good point. Tate knew Donovan didn't do anything because he felt pressured. And he certainly didn't do anything he didn't want to do.

"Do you think I should?"

Reilly answered with, "Do you love him?"

"Yes." Saying it was as natural as breathing. Tate didn't have to wonder or ponder. He loved Donovan and had for a long time.

"Do you see spending your life with him?"

"Yes."

"Then why wait?"

"I don't know."

Reilly sighed. "If you have any doubts—"

"I don't. None at all."

"Then I say go for it, Tate. You can try to outline how it's supposed to work and build a timeline that makes sense, but in the end, if it feels right to both of you, I don't see why you would wait. I mean seriously." Her voice pitched even lower. "Donovan's not gettin' any younger."

Tate barked a laugh. "Neither is Brady."

"I know. That's why I told him I wanted the same thing when he said he wanted to marry me."

Tate gasped, his breath lodged in his throat. He barely contained the squeal of excitement. "He asked you to marry him? Oh, sweetie—"

"He didn't ask," she cut in. "He said he wanted to, but he hasn't actually asked."

But it was coming. Tate knew Brady. The man was like Donovan in the sense he was traditional. Probably wanted to ask for her father's permission first.

"Say yes, Tate," Reilly urged. "Give yourself permission to be happy. You deserve it."

"We both do," he corrected.

"And I think we're both getting exactly what we wanted this Christmas." Reilly chuckled. "I mean, it's not an iPhone or anything…"

Tate laughed, and this time, he knew he hadn't stifled it. A second later, he heard Donovan clearing his throat.

"I gotta go," Reilly said. "Brady just busted me on the phone. I'll talk to you at Mom and Dad's later, right?"

"You definitely will."

Tate ended the call and stood up from where he'd been sitting on the closed toilet lid. He opened the door and saw Donovan standing in the doorway, one shoulder against the wall.

He cut his eyes to the phone. "Reilly?"

Tate nodded.

"Did you have a good chat?"

He nodded again.

"Did she convince you it's okay to say yes?"

Another nod, and this time, he couldn't help but smile.

"Are you sayin' yes, Tate?"

One more nod.

Donovan pushed off the wall, moving toward him.

"Say yes, Tate. I need to hear it."

Tate tilted his head back, holding Donovan's gaze. "Yes. I'll move in with you."

"And when I ask you to marry me, your answer will be…?"

Tate gasped, and his heart felt too large for his chest to contain it.

Donovan laughed. "Don't panic yet." He leaned in and kissed him softly. "Just know it's comin'."

Twenty-Two

"You realize we're gonna be late if you don't get your cute little ass in gear," Donovan called from the living room.

Tate looked in the mirror, trying to figure out why he was so nervous.

He was still staring at his reflection when he heard Donovan's heavy footsteps moving closer. A second later, Donovan appeared behind him. His green eyes were filled with both amusement and concern as he studied Tate.

"You okay?"

Tate nodded, but he didn't move. He couldn't. It was like he was frozen in place; every cell in his body was buzzing, but he wasn't sure how to function with all the rioting in his body. He wouldn't go so far as to say it was fear, but there was some trepidation. He couldn't seem to stop expecting the fallout. This seemed too good to be true, and from experience, whenever it seemed that way, it usually was. Hell, just look at his track record with men. No matter how hard he tried, he could never seem to make a relationship work. And here was the most incredible man he'd ever met, wanting to give him everything he'd ever dreamed of.

It couldn't be that easy, could it?

Donovan moved up behind him. The warmth of his body permeated Tate's as he stood behind him, his big arms coming around him.

Tate wasn't sure he would ever get used to seeing Donovan like this. For so long, it had been a fantasy. It still didn't seem real, and Tate worried that he was going to wake up any minute and find he was alone in his bed, and the past few days had been nothing more than a dream. He didn't want to be dreaming. He wanted this to be real.

As though he sensed Tate was seconds away from having a full-blown panic attack, Donovan's grip on him tightened as he pulled Tate back against him, his arms crossed over Tate's chest. Tate hooked his hands on Donovan's arms and stared at their reflection.

"I love you," Donovan said, his eyes glittering in the vanity lights.

"You do?" *Oh, man. Way to ruin the moment.*

Donovan's smirk was charged with both lust and love. "I realized I've asked you to move in and to marry me, but I haven't told you that yet." His arms tightened a little more. "But that's what this feeling is. It's love. Pure and simple."

Tate stared at him, too stunned to speak.

"We don't have to rush this, Tate. We can take this as slow as you need."

Tate's sinuses burned, and he feared he was about to cry. Somehow, he choked back the emotion long enough to say, "Were you serious?"

"About?"

"Marryin' me."

Donovan's eyes glittered again. "I'll do it tomorrow if you'll say yes."

"Really?"

"Really."

Tate studied Donovan's beautiful face in the mirror, but he wasn't sure what he was looking for.

"I'm scared." The words were out of his mouth before his brain gave them permission.

Donovan didn't appear surprised. "Of?"

"This. You. Me. How do you know it's real?"

"Because I feel it," he said, his arms moving until his hand was over Tate's heart. He tapped his chest twice. "I feel it here."

"You're sure it's not lust?"

"I'm pretty sure I feel that somewhere else."

Tate rolled his eyes because, yeah, now that he thought about it, that was a stupid question.

Donovan chuckled, and his eyes glittered with amusement as he released Tate, but only so he could turn him around.

Tate peered up into Donovan's face, waiting for an explanation that might give him some reassurance that this wasn't going to end in a week and he would be left with a broken heart. He wanted to believe it, but he'd been down this road before and knew he wouldn't survive a broken heart delivered by Donovan Jameson. Tate had never felt anything remotely close to what he felt for this man, and if it didn't work, he was pretty much ruined for life.

"I'm gonna prove it to you," Donovan said, his eyes skimming his face. "We won't have sex for six months."

Tate jerked back. "What?"

Donovan laughed.

Tate realized he was joking, and he exhaled his relief. The thought of spending the next six months without sex with this man was preposterous. Hell, Tate was ready for another round already, but they had somewhere they needed to be. Otherwise, he would've already attempted to seduce this man.

"Fine," Donovan said. "You want sex, we'll have sex."

Tate couldn't help it, he laughed. "I'm serious."

"So am I. But if you want to take this slow, I can do slow. We can date. You can sleep in your bed, I'll sleep in mine. Alone. Cold and alone. No body heat to warm us, no—"

"I see what you're doin'," Tate said with a gruff chuckle, cutting him off as he put his hands on Donovan's hips.

"What am I doin'?"

"You're…" Tate shrugged. "I don't know."

Donovan's laugh was so deep it reverberated through Tate's entire body and lightened something inside him.

But then it stopped, and Donovan cupped his face, staring down at him. "I've never been more serious about anything," he whispered. "The other mornin' … when I woke up in your bed alone, I wasn't pissed that you left. Maybe a little. But more so, I was disappointed that you weren't there. I wanted to open my eyes and see you. I wanted to pull you against me so I could feel you. And yeah, maybe I wanted to get inside you again, but that was secondary.

"I realized then that it wasn't about sex. I wanted _you_, Tate. And fine, maybe I don't know everything about you or vice versa, but I want to learn those things. I don't want to do the dance because I already know that it's love. I want to expand on that. I want to give you everything you could ever want. Me. No one else. I don't see a reason to wait, but I will if that's what you need.

"So, no, you don't have to move in here. We can take this one day at a time. That's fine with me. I know I'm not a patient man. Not when it comes to getting something I want." He leaned down. "But that's because I don't want much, so when I find something—or in this case, some_one_—that I can see myself spending the rest of my life with, I don't want to waste a second. It might not make sense to you that I want to spend every spare second I have with you, but that's okay. You don't have to feel the same. You don't have—"

Tate put his hand over Donovan's mouth. "I love you."

Donovan's smile caused the corners of his eyes to crinkle. "I love you, too." Donovan exhaled heavily. "We do have to table this for a little while, though. We're late as it is."

Tate looked around as though he might find a clock on the bathroom wall. "Oh, shit."

"Yeah. And bein' late means my sister gets first dibs on the pies."

Tate grinned. "She probably hid them already."

"Probably." Donovan stepped back, still holding his gaze. "We good?"

"Yeah. We're good."

And as soon as the words were out of his mouth, Tate realized it was the truth.

WHEN BRADY PULLED THE SUV DOWN HER parents' driveway, Reilly wasn't sure what she was feeling. Giddy? Anxious? Both? For her, the physical sensations were often the same, so she couldn't decipher which emotion churned in her veins. She was feeling something, though.

"You good?"

Her head started bobbing up and down. Yeah. She was good. Definitely that.

"Hey," Brady said as he parked, his hand covering hers to get her attention.

"I love you," she exclaimed, snapping her gaze to his. "I just wanted you to hear it when we weren't ... you know." God, her face was hot. "I love you. I've loved you for a long time, and I know I'll love you even longer. I just—"

He squeezed her hand. "I love you, too."

His tone was as sincere as the love she saw in his eyes, and it made her chest ache. In a good way.

Brady held her gaze as he brushed her hair back from her face, his eyes imploring her.

"I'm nervous," she admitted. "About seeing my parents. About telling them."

"Why?"

She knew he was honestly asking. There was no concern or skepticism in his voice.

"This is different. You and me. Not you and Donovan." She shrugged. "You know what I mean."

He chuckled softly. "Different is okay," he assured her.

"I know." And she did. Mostly.

But what if her parents didn't see this as a good thing? What if they thought she was moving too fast? She didn't think she was, but maybe Tate was right. Maybe it was fast, and they needed to slow down.

Brady cupped her face as he leaned closer. She did the same, kissing him softly. As soon as her lips touched his, all her concerns fell away. It felt right to be with him. She wasn't sure why that was, but it did. It was just that she'd loved him for so long, it was going to take some getting used to. All the hot chocolate wishes in the world would've never prepared her for the actual thrill of knowing this man reciprocated her feelings.

"When we're done here, whenever that is, I'd like you to go back to my house. Or I'll stay at yours. Either way. As long as I get to spend more time with you."

"I'm moving in," she told him.

His eyebrows rose slowly.

"I mean, if that's still what you want."

"More than anything."

"Good because it's not too fast."

"Huh?"

Reilly shook her head. "Nothin'. Sorry. I'm just rambling. But I do want to. Move in with you, I mean. Now. Today, even. I don't care. As long as I get to sleep in the same bed and wake up in the same bed and have breakfast in the same house."

"You're adorable," he whispered.

More like neurotic, but Reilly wasn't going to argue.

Brady took a breath and sat back in his seat. "What do you say we go inside? I'm sure your mom and dad are watchin' from the window."

She figured they were, too. That was how it worked on holidays. Her parents waited patiently for everyone to arrive, but their patience had limits. They usually paced back and forth in front of the windows, watching for their kids to come home.

Sure enough, as soon as she was out of the truck, her dad appeared on the front porch, a mug in his hand and a smile on his face.

"I was startin' to think we were gonna have dinner in your car," Owen said as they approached, Brady moving closer to her as they walked.

"Hi, Daddy," she greeted, hugging him.

"Hi, sugar." Owen released her. "Where's Tate?"

"With Donovan," she said without thinking about it.

Her father grinned, then opened the screen door to allow her to go inside.

Reilly stopped as soon as she was in the house, eyes wide as she stared at the ceiling.

"What did you do?" she asked, huffing a laugh as she noticed all the mistletoe dangling from the ceiling. They'd taken down hers because it would've been dead at this point, but every sprig had been replaced with new ones, only there was twice—no, make that three times as much.

Her dad stood beside her, admiring his handiwork. "Your mom and I thought we'd pitch in and help you kids out." He glanced at Brady. "I didn't realize you boys had gotten with the program."

Reilly looked at Brady, noticed there was color in his cheeks. He was blushing.

"Yes, sir," he said. "With that said, if you've got a minute, I'd like to talk to you about somethin'."

Unable to move, Reilly watched them until her dad looked at her and smiled. "Go on in the kitchen. Your mama's waitin' for you."

She was torn between helping her mom and lingering so she could hear what Brady wanted to talk to him about.

Brady made her decision for her when he leaned over and whispered in her ear. "Go on. We'll be there in a minute."

She met his gaze, held it as she tried to read his intentions. Her stomach was churning, and this time, it was excitement. "Okay."

It took effort to contain it as she watched her dad and Brady go out onto the front porch.

"Hey, squirt! Where're you at?" CJ shouted from the kitchen.

Reilly spun around, feeling lighter than she ever had, as she practically skipped to the kitchen.

"Hey," she greeted her brother.

"What's up, kid?" he replied, not looking up from his phone.

"Hi, Mama!" she chirped, circling the island so she could hug her mother.

"Hi, honey." Deborah looked at her, skimming her face, cataloging her mood as always. "You look happy."

"That doesn't begin to describe it," she said, barely containing all the joy that filled her as she wrapped her arms around her mother. "He loves me," she whispered.

Expecting her mother to ask her who she was referring to, Reilly was shocked when her mother said, "I've known that for a while. What took *you* so long to figure it out?"

"Yeah," CJ added. "What she said."

Reilly pulled back and looked her mother in the eye. She was smiling brightly. So brightly tears formed in Reilly's eyes.

Of course she knew. Her mother knew everything. She always had.

"You know what my next question is gonna be, don't you?" Deborah asked.

Reilly's eyebrows lifted. "What?"

Her mother leaned close and lowered her voice. "It's gonna be a big wedding, right?"

That giddy sensation intensified. So powerful it was a wonder Reilly didn't shatter into a million bright, sparkling lights.

Twenty-Three

"IF YOU'RE ABOUT TO ASK ME WHAT I think you're about to ask me…"

Brady heard the concern in Owen's voice, but surprisingly, it didn't cause him to second-guess himself.

"I—"

Owen stopped him by holding up a hand and standing directly in front of him.

"Do you love her?"

Brady's breath caught. Considering how quickly things escalated between him and Reilly, Brady hadn't anticipated her father to expect him to ask for permission to marry her.

"Yes, sir," he said because that was the truth.

"Then, as long as you make each other happy, you have our blessing."

"Thank you, sir. Honestly, I thought you'd have concerns about how long we've been seein' each other."

"Oh, you mean the fact that you didn't get with the program until the last few days?" Owen chuckled. "Sure, it's fast. But I know you, Brady. And I trust you. You won't do anything until you're absolutely sure it's right for both of you." Owen's expression sobered. "I can't imagine a better man for my daughter." He gestured toward the house. "Don't think I'm oblivious. I know she put all that mistletoe up for you."

Brady grinned.

"And so we're clear. We put the mistletoe up for the same reason. Figured we might help you kids along, but it looks like you don't need the help."

"No, sir. Reilly has a way of makin' a man see reason," Brady told him.

"That she does. Does Donovan know?"

"Yeah. I called him this mornin'."

Owen jerked his chin toward the driveway. "Keep in mind, she's got two other brothers."

Brady glanced out to see Stone pulling down the driveway. "I haven't forgotten."

And that was true. Brady had already talked to Donovan because he owed his best friend that much. And he'd wanted to get Owen's blessing, not just to marry her but also to ensure the man knew he was serious about her. He intended to give Stone and CJ the same respect. The Jamesons were a protective bunch. He knew because he was as much a part of their family as any of the kids. The last thing he would ever do was cause problems for them.

Not that Reilly would let them. She would no doubt put her brothers in their place if they thought for one second they could tell her how to live her life. But Brady knew how much they meant to her. And to him.

So here he was.

As Stone was parking, another car pulled in behind him—Chelsea and Paul—and then Donovan's truck appeared a moment later.

"What do you say we get this crew inside and eat?" Owen told him.

"Sounds like a good idea to me."

Because he knew Owen liked to greet his kids separately, Brady slipped into the house and headed for the kitchen. Reilly was helping her mother arrange the food on the counters.

CJ was the first to greet him, holding up his fist to bump. Brady returned it.

As soon as Deborah saw him, she pulled off her oven mitts and came around the island to give him a hug.

"Merry Christmas," she said.

"Merry Christmas."

When she pulled back, she took his hands and held them in both of hers. "Eve is smilin' up there right now."

The mention of his mother had emotion clogging his throat. He wished she was here because, yes, he knew she would've been beside herself at the idea of him and Reilly together. The only thing his mother ever wanted was for him to be happy. He was. More so than he'd ever been in his life.

"You good?" Reilly asked, coming over to stand by him.

He nodded as Deborah released his hands. When Reilly walked into his arms, he held onto her and smiled to himself. Yeah. No doubt his mother was smiling.

"Do you know if Tate's out there?" Reilly asked, looking up at him while her arms were still around his waist.

"He is."

She stepped back and huffed, her smile radiant. "Oh, thank God. I thought for a minute they were gonna bail."

"What in the Christmas miracle is goin' on in here?" Stone asked, making his way past them and over to his mother. "I just saw Donovan and Tate gettin' outta the same truck."

Reilly giggled. "They love each other."

Stone smiled even as his gaze slid to Brady. "It seems to be in the water."

He definitely hadn't missed the fact that Brady had been hugging Reilly.

"Yeah." Brady nodded as he looked at Reilly. "It definitely is."

"And here I was thinkin' *my* news was gonna be big."

CJ looked up from his phone.

Reilly's hand paused as she set the butter dish beside the rolls.

Deborah stopped what she was doing, her eyes wide. "What news?"

Everyone stared at Stone, waiting for his big announcement.

Stone grinned, slowly skimming every face in the room. "I'm movin' back to Coyote Ridge."

Deborah clasped her hands together as tears formed in her eyes. "Really?"

Reilly squealed and ran over to hug him. Stone put one arm around her and the other around his mother, hugging them both as he smiled.

Brady was curious what had happened, but he decided not to voice the question. He figured that information would come soon enough. In the meantime, the fact that he was moving back was all that really mattered.

"You can live in the barn," Reilly told him.

"I might have to take you up on that."

"Tears?" Donovan asked when he joined them, his gaze coming to rest on Stone. "You told 'em?"

"I did," Stone confirmed.

It didn't surprise Brady that Donovan was in the know. The man kept his thumb on the pulse of his siblings. That had always been the case.

Deborah wiped her eyes as she pulled away, giggling before she went over and hugged Tate and Donovan.

"Does a girl hafta go into labor to get some attention?" Chelsea asked when she came into the room.

Brady stepped back, allowing everyone to fit in the space.

"What did I miss?" Chelsea asked as she hugged her mom.

"Stone's movin' home," Deborah announced, still wiping tears away. "Brady and Reilly are gettin' married. One day," she tacked on with a giggle. "And Donovan and Tate are movin' in together."

"Oh, we're gettin' married, too," Donovan noted as he put his arm around Tate. "When he's ready."

Tate blushed, shaking his head as though he couldn't believe Donovan had said that.

Chelsea's eyes were wide as she looked around at each of them. "What the hell?" She looked at her husband. "We were here a week ago, right?"

"More like three weeks," Reilly said with a laugh.

"Fine. Three weeks and..." Chelsea shook her head, disbelief etched on her pretty face. "Wow." She looked at Brady. "It's about damn time."

That caught him off guard. "What?"

Chelsea looked at Donovan. "The same goes for you."

"What did I do?"

"For someone who knows everything, you're kinda oblivious."

Brady looked at Donovan. What was she talking about?

Chelsea grinned. "My little sister's been in love with you"—she pointed at Brady—"and Tate's been in love with you"—she pointed at Donovan—"for so long. I thought y'all would *never* figure it out."

Brady looked at Reilly, warmth filling in his chest. "She opened my eyes."

"She has a way of doin' that," Donovan chimed in.

Reilly nodded. "I'm good. What can I say?"

"So no more hot chocolate wishes?" Deborah asked, looking at all her kids.

"Oh, there'll definitely be more," Tate answered.

"Yeah," Reilly chimed in. "But we won't be wishin' for iPhones anymore."

Brady chuckled. God, he loved this adorable woman.

TWO HOURS LATER, AS EVERYONE REMAINED AT the dining room table chatting about anything and everything, Donovan excused himself so he could start working on the dishes. It was tradition. His mother cooked, and the kids cleaned. And if he expected to get Tate home anytime in the near future, it had to be done.

"You want help in there?" Stone asked.

"No," he said, meaning it. "I've got this."

"Really?" Reilly asked, looking sincerely concerned.

Donovan grinned. "I'll even put on some coffee."

"You know we're not gonna argue, right?" Stone commented.

Donovan chuckled. "It's easier if y'all stay outta the kitchen."

"I'll help," Tate offered, pushing back from the table.

"You're not gonna tell him no, huh?" CJ teased.

"Not a chance." Donovan looked at Tate. "I'll take his help anytime."

Donovan wasn't about to turn down a few minutes alone with Tate. Anything that would allow him to get his hands on the man. Even if for only a minute.

"Y'all head to the livin' room," Reilly told everyone. "I'll help them clear the table."

"Don't have to tell me twice," Chelsea said as she pushed to her feet, her husband helping her up.

While everyone started moving around, Donovan headed for the sink and flipped on the faucet. The dishes were scattered throughout the kitchen and dining room, but it wouldn't take long to get it under control. As was the saying, this wasn't Donovan's first rodeo. He knew all it took was for him to make the suggestion, and everyone else would start helping so that they could get the dirty part out of the way and move on to the good stuff. Which for them happened to be unwrapping all those gifts under the tree.

Brady joined a moment later. As did Reilly.

Tate came over to start loading the dishwasher as Donovan rinsed everything, setting aside the largest items to be hand-washed when the dishwasher was full.

Five minutes later, Reilly returned with the last stack of plates and silverware. "This is the last of 'em. You sure you don't want help?"

"We've got this," Donovan assured her.

As soon as she left and he was finally alone with Tate, Donovan turned off the water and grabbed a hand towel.

"There's still room for—"

Before Tate could finish that sentence, Donovan had him backed up against the counter, tipping his chin up with his fingertip so he could kiss him.

"Mmm," Tate moaned as Donovan pulled him in close.

Footsteps sounded as someone approached, but Donovan didn't stop kissing Tate to see who it was. A moment later, the footsteps receded.

"They need a minute," CJ announced, followed by a round of laughter.

Donovan smiled against Tate's mouth. "You're not embarrassed, are you?"

Tate had a firm grip on Donovan's shirt. "Surprisingly, no."

"Good." He kissed him again, reining himself in a little. "Because I'm not."

Tate smiled up at him. "This has been the best Christmas."

"I won't disagree."

They stared at one another for a moment, and Donovan swiped his thumb along Tate's cheek.

"I won't pretend I don't wanna take you home, though."

Tate's smile widened. "And I won't pretend I don't want to go home. You still sure you want me there?"

"I've never been more sure about anything in my life."

As he stared at this man, Donovan felt so much, it was nearly overwhelming. He honestly never expected to feel this way again. More shocking than that was the fact that Tate had been right there all along. As much as he wanted to speed up this process, he knew Tate was right to slow things down. But Donovan had no doubts at all. Not a single one. He knew exactly what he wanted, and he was going to do whatever it took to make it happen.

More specifically, he would do whatever it took to make Tate happy because having the man in his life was the best gift he could've ever been given. He damn sure wasn't going to let the opportunity for a happily ever after pass him by.

"All right, you two! Quit makin' out! It's time to open presents," Reilly shouted.

Color infused Tate's cheeks.

"Let's get the gifts outta the way so I can take you home and unwrap you," Donovan whispered before kissing Tate one more time.

"What if I wanted to do the unwrapping part?"

Donovan stepped back and stared down at this man who had suddenly become the best part of his existence. "Baby, I'll let you have anything you want. Just say the word."

Acknowledgments

So *that* happened.

When I sat down to write this story, I thought it would be one of my Naughty Holidays books. I figured a short novella and it would be a fun, hot way to spend the holidays. Then I got to know the Jamesons, and I realized there was a lot more to get to know about the family that makes up such a large part of the small town of Coyote Ridge. And yes, there are as many members of this family tree as there are Walkers, so I think it's going to get interesting. I hope you're looking forward to the next one.

Now for my thanks…

My husband is always at the top of the list because he allows me to live my dream, and he has dinner with me every night, even if he thinks I might spend too much time talking to imaginary people. I'm okay with that as long as I don't have to cook.

Next is Chancy Powley and Jenna Underwood. Our friendship is something I will never take for granted. I might not be the best at relaying how I feel but know that I think the world of you both. Thank you. Those two little words will never relay how much I appreciate your friendship.

Nicole Nation 2.0, for the constant support and love and for those of you who have my back. You've been there for me from almost the beginning. This group of ladies has kept me going for so long that I'm not sure I'd know what to do without them.

And, of course, YOU, the reader. Your emails, messages, posts, comments … they mean more to me than you can imagine. I thrive on hearing from you; knowing that my characters and stories have touched you somehow keeps me going. I've been known to shed a tear or two when reading an email because your support brings so much joy to my life. I thank you for that.

ABOUT NICOLE EDWARDS

New York Times and *USA Today* bestselling author Nicole Edwards lives in the suburbs of Austin, Texas, with her husband, their three fur babies, and the youngest of their three children, who has threatened never to leave home. When Nicole is not writing about sexy alpha males and sassy, independent women, she can often be found with a book in hand or attempting to keep the dogs happy. You can find her hanging out on social media and interacting with her readers - even when she's supposed to be writing.

Connect with Nicole

I hope you're as eager to get the information as I am to give it. Any of these things is worth signing up for, or feel free to sign up for all. I do my best to keep each one unique and interesting.

NIC NEWS - If you haven't signed up for my newsletter and want notifications regarding preorders, new releases, giveaways, sales, etc., then you'll want to sign up. I promise not to spam your email, just get you the most important updates.

RAMBLINGS OF A WRITER BLOG - My blog is used for writer ramblings, which I am known to do from time to time.

NICOLE NATION - Visit my website to find exclusive content you won't find anywhere else, including Sneak Peeks, A Day in the Life character stories, exclusive giveaways, cards from Nicole, and join Nicole's review team.

NICOLE NATION ON FACEBOOK - Join my Facebook reader group to interact with other readers, ask me questions, play fun weekly games, celebrate during release week, and enter exclusive giveaways!

INSTAGRAM - Basically, Instagram is where I post pictures of my dogs, so if you want to see epic cuteness, you should follow me.

NAUGHTY & NICE SHOP - Not only does the shop have signed books, but there's fun merchandise, too—plenty of naughty and nice options to go around.

You can also follow Nicole on Facebook | Instagram | TikTok | BookBub | Goodreads

AUSTIN ARROWS
Rush
Kaufman

CLUB DESTINY
Conviction
Temptation
Addicted
Seduction
Infatuation
Captivated
Devotion
Perception
Entrusted
Adored
Distraction
Forevermore

DEAD HEAT RANCH
Boots Optional
Betting on Grace
Overnight Love
Jared (a crossover novel)

DEVIL'S BEND
Chasing Dreams
Vanishing Dreams

MISPLACED HALOS
Protected in Darkness
Salvation in Darkness
Bound in Darkness

OFFICE INTRIGUE
Office Intrigue
Intrigued Out of The Office
Their Rebellious Submissive
Their Famous Dominant
Their Ruthless Sadist
Their Naughty Student
Their Fairy Princess
Owned

PIER 70
Reckless
Fearless
Speechless
Harmless
Clueless

PRIMAL INSTINCTS
Chase (Volume 1-3)
Capture (Volume 4-6)
Claim (Volume 7-9)

SNIPER 1 SECURITY
Wait for Morning
Never Say Never
Tomorrow's Too Late

SOUTHERN BOY MAFIA/DEVIL'S PLAYGROUND
Beautifully Brutal
Without Regret
Beautifully Loyal
Without Restraint

STANDALONE NOVELS
Unhinged Trilogy
A Million Tiny Pieces
Inked on Paper
Bad Reputation
Bad Business
Filthy Hot Billionaire

NAUGHTY HOLIDAY EDITIONS
2015
2016
2021